——————

....

....

....

....

....

....

....

....

....

....

....

....

....

....

....

....
Pleas
sh.

Oh, God, he was planning to kiss her, and if he did she'd kiss him back. She knew she would.

'You said you weren't interested.'

'I lied. I'm interested.'

'No,' she breathed, managing to sound outraged, sexy and needy all at the same time—which so wasn't the plan.

'Why not?'

'I never mix business with pleasure,' she said, focusing on one of the founding principles of her company, albeit a bit belatedly.

'Neither do I. But the party's over and we no longer have business together.'

'We might. Hopefully.'

'What does that have to do with now?' he asked, his gaze roaming slowly, sensuously, over her features. 'All I'm suggesting is a kiss.'

Yeah, right. Like they'd stop at a kiss. Like she'd be able to. A kiss would be the beginning.

Dear Reader,

THE PARTY STARTS AT MIDNIGHT is one of two books that feature a couple of property tycoon brothers. Both are gorgeous (naturally!) but very different. Leo—the numbers man—is dark and serious, while Jake—the 'face' of the company—is more of a charmer.

First up is Leo, whose calm, ordered life is just as he likes it. Until, that is, he meets events planner Abby Summers—and from that moment on he's in a complete spin. As a perfectionist, career-driven Abby's none too happy about the chaos Leo brings to her thought processes either.

I loved the idea of two people who think they have life sussed and then, like two hydrogen atoms crashing together with a whole lot of heat—*boom!*—realise they so very clearly don't. Talk about chemistry…*phew!*

I hope that you love it too.

Lucy x

THE PARTY STARTS AT MIDNIGHT

BY
LUCY KING

First published in Great Britain 2014
by Mills & Boon, an imprint of Harlequin (UK) Limited,
Eton House, 18-24 Paradise Road, Richmond, Surrey, TW9 1SR

© 2014 Lucy King

ISBN: 978-0-263-24312-3

Harlequin (UK) Limited's policy is to use papers that are natural,
renewable and recyclable products and made from wood grown in
sustainable forests. The logging and manufacturing processes conform
to the legal environmental regulations of the country of origin.

Printed and bound in Great Britain
by CPI Antony Rowe, Chippenham, Wiltshire

Lucy King spent her formative years lost in the world of Mills & Boon® romance when she really ought to have been paying attention to her teachers. Up against sparkling heroines, gorgeous heroes and the magic of falling in love, trigonometry and absolute ablatives didn't stand a chance.

But as she couldn't live in a dream world for ever she eventually acquired a degree in languages and an eclectic collection of jobs. A stroll to the River Thames one Saturday morning led her to her very own hero. The minute she laid eyes on the hunky rower getting out of a boat, clad only in Lycra and carrying a three-metre oar as if it was a toothpick, she knew she'd met the man she was going to marry. Luckily the rower thought the same.

She will always be grateful to whatever it was that made her stop dithering and actually sit down to type Chapter One, because dreaming up her own sparkling heroines and gorgeous heroes is pretty much her idea of the perfect job.

Originally a Londoner, Lucy now lives in Spain, where she spends much of her time reading, failing to finish cryptic crosswords, and trying to convince herself that lying on the beach really *is* the best way to work.

Visit her at www.lucykingbooks.com

Other Modern Tempted™ titles by Lucy King:

THE BEST MAN FOR THE JOB
ONE NIGHT WITH HER EX
THE REUNION LIE

DEDICATION

To my wonderful readers,
without whom I couldn't do a job I love.

CHAPTER ONE

As the lift doors opened with an expensively soft swoosh, Abby gave her head a quick shake to dispel the ear-popping dizziness caused by the thirty-floors-in-three-seconds ascension, and stepped into the hall of the penthouse suite of London's newest South Bank hotel.

'Hello?' she called, her voice ringing out weirdly loudly in the silence of the apartment. And then, after a moment during which there was no answer, she tried again. 'Mr Cartwright?...Leo?...Anyone?'

But there was still no reply.

Frowning slightly, she headed down the hall, barely noticing the thick cream carpet her heels were sinking into or the cool sophistication of the dove-grey walls that stretched out either side of her, and came upon the sitting room. A quick scan showed it to be huge and beautifully furnished but disappointingly empty, as, she subsequently discovered, were the kitchen, laundry room, library, cinema, gym and study.

If she hadn't been on a mission to locate the man allegedly holed up within and remind him about the party in full swing downstairs—the party he was supposed to be attending but wasn't—Abby might have been blown away by the sheer scale and luxury of the place.

She might have ditched her precious clipboard and marvelled at the spectacular view of London at night, all lit up like the enormous Christmas tree that sat in the lobby downstairs, and showcased by the acres of window. She might have oohed and aahed over the gorgeous chrome-and-crystal chandeliers that hung from the ceiling and cast subtle light over the antiques, and then thrown herself onto one of the three plush, charcoal velvet-covered sofas with a sigh of pleasure.

She might have lingeringly run her fingers along the gleaming granite work surfaces in the kitchen, had a quick go on one of the many machines in the state-of-the-art gym or wondered about the nearly empty bottle of whisky that sat on the desk in the study and the glass that lay on its side on a messy pile of faintly stained papers beside it.

As it was, she didn't have either the time or the inclination to gawp, cop a feel or wonder about the possible evidence of a drinking session because the sumptuousness of his home wasn't important right now. What *was* important was that Leo Cartwright was meant to be downstairs and she was here to fetch him.

If only she could find him.

Still in the study Abby put down her clipboard, and, out of habit, picked up the glass and put it on a coaster she saw peeping out from beneath a book. Then shuffled the papers into a neat pile.

She had to admit that despite Jake's assurance that his brother was definitely up here, the silence and general air of absence didn't bode particularly well.

And OK, so there was still the bedroom/bathroom half of the flat that she hadn't searched, but there was no way she was heading in that direction. It was bad enough that she was in Leo's flat uninvited in the first place, and, even though Jake had said he'd take full responsibility for any outcome, she absolutely drew the line at scouring the bedrooms without some kind of authorisation at least.

Perching on the edge of the desk, she took her phone out of the discreet little pouch sewn into the inside of her belt and scrolled down until she came to Jake's number. She hit the dial button, waited for a second and then, when he picked up, said, 'Jake, I'm afraid there's no sign of him.'

'What, nowhere?' came the deep voice at the other end of the line.

'Not that I can see. Are you sure he's up here?'

'About ninety-nine per cent. He was when I last spoke to him. Where have you looked?'

'Everywhere,' she said, then added, 'Well, everywhere apart from the bedrooms.'

There was a pause while he wished someone a happy Christmas and told them to grab a glass of champagne, and then he was back. 'Why haven't you checked the bedrooms?'

'It seemed like an invasion of privacy,' she said, thinking that actually, talking of privacy, if Leo *was* in there, he could well be doing something that meant he either hadn't been able to hear her calling or didn't want to. Possibly something wholly absorbing and *very* private indeed.

'You needn't worry about interrupting anything,' said Jake, now sounding a bit impatient and, apparently, able to read her mind. 'It's seven in the evening and besides, Leo hasn't had a woman in his bed for years.'

Which was way more than she needed to know about anyone, let alone a client. 'Nevertheless, I—'

'Look, Abby,' said Jake, cutting across her protest in an I'm-the-client-here tone that told her he'd had enough and would brook no further argument. 'I have to make this speech, and people are wondering where he is—as am I—so will you please just go and see if you can find him?'

Realising this wasn't a battle she was going to win and consoling herself with the thought that so far they'd actually been remarkably—and surprisingly, given their exacting standards—easy clients, Abby gave in. After all, it was hardly the worst thing she'd been asked to do in her ten years of event planning, was it? The Cartwright brothers were paying her a lot of money to ensure that this evening went smoothly and if that meant that Leo Cartwright had to be located, then locate him she would. Wherever he was and whatever he was doing.

And so what if he had the faintly intimidating reputation of being formidable, ruthless and utterly devoid of emotion? He couldn't be any trickier to handle than the last client she'd had, could he? She'd take cold, formidable and ruthless over a bad-tempered paranoid who'd accused her at virtually every meeting of, at best, wasting his money, at worst, siphoning some of it off.

'Sure,' she said briskly, mentally pulling on her big-girl pants and injecting steel into her spine. 'No problem.'

'Thanks,' said Jake, and cut the call.

Swiping at her phone to lock the screen, Abby put it away and pushed herself off the desk. Then she smoothed her dress and adjusted her belt so that the bright silver bow once again sat exactly above her left hip bone.

Really, there was no need to feel awkward or uncomfortable or nervous about searching the rest of the flat, was there? She was just doing her job. She'd call ahead—loudly—and if Leo was in there he'd be alerted to her presence. He'd call back, she'd retreat and wait, and everything would be absolutely fine. There'd be no unwelcome surprises. No embarrassing moments. No inappropriate or foolish behaviour.

Satisfied with the plan, she checked her chignon for hair that might have escaped the pins, and then, pleased to find nothing amiss, picked up her clipboard and set off to investigate.

And while stomping to announce her arrival was never going to work given the deadening effect of the thick deep-pile carpet, perhaps a loud cheery hello would.

'Hello, hello,' she called brightly, and stuck her head round the door to a huge, immaculate but empty bedroom before moving to the next. 'Anyone home?' she trilled, but her quarry wasn't there either.

Nor—perhaps thankfully—did she find him in the gorgeous bathroom that was practically the size of the ground floor of her house or, unsurprisingly enough, in the laundry cupboard.

Which left only one room to try.

Standing at the entrance to what she presumed was the master bedroom suite and her last hope, she listened for a moment for sounds that suggested he might be engaged in an activity she'd rather not disturb.

Blessedly hearing none, she rapped on the door that was ajar, and then, after taking a deep breath, went in.

And there he was.

Alone, thank goodness. But lying flat out on his back, sprawled diagonally across the bed, naked apart from a perilously small section of white bunched-up sheet that loosely covered him from waist to mid-thigh, and illuminated by a pool of soft light cast by the bedside lamp.

For one frozen heart-stopping moment Abby couldn't work out what to do next. Which was odd because she always had a plan. Always. More than one, in fact; when it came to the events she organised she had plans to cover every imaginable eventuality. Her job, her success, depended on it, and so she never didn't know what to do.

But now, as she looked at him, strangely unable to drag her gaze away, her mouth going dry and her heart thumping unnaturally fast, she couldn't even *think*, let alone act because for some unfathomable reason her brain appeared to be having a bit of a wiring problem. Alarmingly, rational thought was heading for the hills. Her common sense was evaporating. And her unfailing capability to do her job was, well, for the first time in years, apparently *failing*.

The fast-disappearing professional side of her was dimly aware she should go and shake him awake and point out that he was late for his own party. But the sometime insomniac in her wanted to leave him to sleep, and the woman in her—who hadn't been up close and personal to a man in six

months and was now very much making herself known—
was quite happy to just stand there and ogle for as long as it
took him to wake up. Because with the broad muscled shoulders, the tanned hair-sprinkled chest and the long powerful
legs that suggested the gym wasn't just for show, Leo Cartwright was quite a sight.

Yet as she looked and dithered, the part of her that de-
voured TV hospital dramas began to wonder at the utter
stillness of him, at the strong smell of stale alcohol that was
wafting towards her and the absence of any rise and fall to
his chest.

And it was this that made her brain *finally* engage, because, oh heavens, what if, by some horrible twist of fate,
he weren't simply asleep?

Propelled by a sudden surge of alarm and now no longer
ogling, Abby sprang into action. Not bothering to weave her
way through the clothes that were lying scattered all over
the floor but instead ploughing straight through them and
hardly even noticing, she reached the bed, dropped to her
knees and leaned in close.

With the focus that had had her business making a profit
in its first six months of operation she blanked out the horrible smell, the spark of sexual attraction and the nauseat-
ing panic. Everything, in fact, but the need to find out if he
was OK.

As her pulse galloped she fixed her gaze on his mouth.
Strained her ears. Waited. Listened…

And, after a couple of long heart-thumping seconds, was
able to make out the very faint hiss of breath. Then, as she
looked down, the beat of the pulse at the base of his neck,
barely perceptible, but there.

Oh, thank goodness for that, she thought, sitting back on
her heels and letting out a long slow breath of her own as
the panic subsided and her heart rate returned to normal.

He wasn't dead. Of course he wasn't. He'd merely passed

out, that was all. Which was *such* a relief, not least because while she might be a fan of TV hospital dramas she didn't have the first clue about resuscitation apart from the fact that mouth-to-mouth was no longer thought to be necessary.

And wasn't that a shame, because now she wasn't watching it for signs of life she could see he had a great mouth. Well defined. Sexy.

Much like the rest of his face, she thought, her gaze drifting over his features. His nose was straight and his jaw firm. His cheekbones were sharp and his brows were as thick and dark as the tousled hair on his head. She could only guess at the colour of his eyes but his eyelashes were the kind that a woman who was sometimes strawberry blonde, sometimes ginger, and so had virtually invisible eyelashes, could only dream about.

It was a strong face. Gorgeous. And in sleep there didn't seem anything cold, forbidding or ruthless about him at all. There certainly didn't seem anything cold about his mouth. It looked warm. Soft. Lovely. Tempting. Very, very kissable, and there for the taking.

And whether it was because she'd just had the fright of her life and all kinds of emotions were rushing through her or whether it was because it had been so long since she'd been this close to a man she didn't know, but for one crazy moment she wanted to lean forwards and take. Desperately.

At the thought of it, the intoxicating possibility of it, her head swam and her heart pounded and she very nearly did exactly that. Would have done had not the reason and common sense that had been eluding her slammed back into her head, making her freeze and jerk back as if suddenly jabbed with a red-hot poker because, oh, goodness, she'd actually started *moving.*

What the *hell* was she doing? she wondered, horror at her lack of control shooting through her. What was she thinking? Was she *completely insane*?

This wasn't some kind of gender-reversed Sleeping flipping Beauty. Leo Cartwright wasn't a prince. He was a client. One of her biggest to date, in fact. What if he'd woken up and found her leaning in for a kiss? He'd have been horrified. Appalled. Rightly so. He'd probably have fired her. Her reputation would have been in tatters, her career over, and the blood, sweat, tears and money she'd poured into the business would have been for nothing.

Abby shuddered as an icy sweat broke out all over her skin. God, it didn't bear thinking about. Everything she'd worked for. Possibly gone. In a nanosecond of utter lunacy.

But it was fine, she assured herself, taking a deep calming breath and feeling the nausea churning around in her stomach subside. It had been a close call but she'd pulled herself back from the brink of madness and he hadn't woken up. She'd got away with it. He'd never know what she'd so very nearly done. No one would. It was fine.

And so was she. She had to be. Because she was at work, for heaven's sake. Work. So now wasn't the time for panic, desire and random acts of insanity. In fact, now wasn't the time to be anything other than Abby Summers, event planner extraordinaire. Professional, in control, and completely on top of him—*things*. God. On top of *things*.

Swallowing hard and ruthlessly ignoring the bolt of heat that rocketed through her at the thought of *that*, Abby gave herself a mental slap and pulled herself together because, really, this had to stop. It was ridiculous. *She* was ridiculous. And, quite frankly, she'd had enough.

So she yanked her shoulders back, set her jaw, scanned his upper body for a suitable target and absolutely did *not* think about how it might feel to run her fingers over his chest, his abdomen, maybe following the trail of her hands with her mouth, down, towards the sheet and then lower...

She blinked and snapped her gaze up. His arm would do.

Right. She flexed her hands, leaned forwards and gave his biceps a quick prod.

'Mr Cartwright,' she murmured, her voice sounding unusually husky and weirdly seductive. 'Leo.'

He grunted and shifted but he didn't wake, and, remembering the bottle in the study, Abby wondered how much he'd had to drink. Then she cleared her throat, put her hand flat on his shoulder and, ignoring the heat of his skin and the hardness of his muscle beneath her palm, said his name again. But this time it was loudly and not in the least bit seductively, and the shake she gave him could have roused an elephant.

Which seemed to do the trick because with a bellow that made her nearly topple backwards in fright he twisted round, thrashed about a bit, then jackknifed up.

And just when she thought that the situation couldn't get any worse, just when she thought her body had undergone enough physical wrangling for one evening, there went the sheet.

Abby's gaze automatically shot down his chest to his partially exposed and—oh, Lord—very aroused crotch and, with a strangled yelp, she clapped her hand to her eyes, and thought with the one brain cell that hadn't yet shut down in defeat, no unwelcome surprises? No embarrassing moments? And no inappropriate or foolish behaviour? Hah, who had she been kidding?

A second ago Leo had been asleep. That much he knew. Now he wasn't. That much he knew too. Which was a shame because he'd been having the best dream about a warm woman who smelt of flowers and who'd been leaning over him, murmuring his name and—rather randomly but pleasingly—been just about to kiss him.

But something had disturbed him. Jolted him and roused him to the extent that he was now sitting bolt upright in bed, his pulse racing, his instincts dazed and confused and adrenalin shooting through his blood.

He raked his hands through his hair and gave his head a shake but it didn't dispel the sleep-induced fuzziness, the bewilderment or the thundering of his heart.

What the hell had happened? he wondered dizzily. What had woken him? Not a nightmare, that was for sure. So had it been a noise? A movement? What?

Rolling his shoulders, Leo blinked once, twice, rubbed his gritty eyes with the heels of his hands as he struggled to work it out, and then, quite suddenly, he froze. His entire body tensed and his ears pricked because, hang on, what on earth was that?

It sounded like a breath. To his left. Being released, slowly, carefully, lengthily, as if the owner didn't want him to hear, and ending in a sigh, a whimper, or maybe a moan.

Whatever it was, with the adrenalin still pumping through his veins, preparing his body and mind for fight, Leo dropped his hands and snapped his head round. And nearly leapt a foot in the air because there beside his bed, sitting back on her heels with one hand clamped over her eyes and the other clasped to her chest, was a woman. Slim, reddish-blonde and wearing a dark blue dress with a bow thing tied round her waist. Unknown, uninvited and apparently in as much shock as he was.

Glancing down and seeing the dramatic effect that the dream he'd been having had had on him—which was presumably the reason she'd covered her eyes and explained the harsh, ragged breathing that was making her chest heave—Leo grabbed the sheet and yanked it over his lap.

'Who the hell are you?' he snapped, his voice rough with sleep and astonishment.

'Abby Summers,' she said quickly, hoarsely.

The name didn't ring any bells, but then maybe that wasn't surprising because nothing was ringing any bells right now apart from the fact that he was naked and not alone. 'What are you doing in my bedroom?'

'Looking for you.'

'On your knees?'

'Long story,' she said. 'Not important.'

Wasn't it? Who knew? Leo could barely think straight, let alone work out what might or might not be of importance here. He was too busy processing the fact that there was a strange woman in his bedroom, on the floor with her eyes covered and her breath coming in tiny gasps, making him think of blindfolds and what her gasps might turn into if he suggested she join him actually on the bed instead of beside it. All of which was so unbelievably out of character, so wholly inappropriate and so crazily beyond the realms of his usually rock-solid self-control, his brain would have reeled had it been up to it.

'How did you get in?' he muttered, totally thrown by how badly he wanted to grab her and roll her beneath him when he knew absolutely nothing about her or why she was here, and thinking that, damn, that dream had a lot to answer for.

'The lift.'

'It's locked.'

'Your brother gave me his key card.'

His brother? Huh? *Now* what was going on? Leo rubbed a hand over his face in an effort to wake himself up and get a grip on things. 'Jake did?'

'Yes.' She nodded and the light caught her hair, making it glint gold—no, copper—no, gold—and, momentarily distracted, he wondered what it would be like to pull it down and run his fingers through it. If it would feel as silky and soft as it looked. How many words there were to describe its colour.

Flexing his fingers, then folding his arms and shoving his hands into his armpits just in case they got ideas, Leo hauled his concentration—such as it was—back on track. 'Why?'

'So I could come up and find you, of course,' she said as if it couldn't be clearer, which it wasn't.

But the mention of his brother seemed to have triggered his memory because snippets of the last conversation he and Jake had had were filtering into his head, slowly lifting the fog of confusion and, ah-h-h, now it was all becoming clear.

The time of year.

His mood.

The mention his brother had made of a gift.

Evidently Jake had followed up on his promise, and therefore Leo knew *exactly* who Abby Whoever-She-Was was, and what she was here for.

'Right,' he muttered, not really up to working out how he felt about what his brother had done. 'I get it. You're here to cheer me up.'

There was a pause, during which he watched her mouth open, close, then open again to emit a slightly startled, 'What?'

'Jake said he was going to send me something to make me feel better,' he said flatly. 'And here you are, all dressed up like a gift. In my bedroom. Virtually in my bed. So who are you? Someone who owes him a favour? One of his desperate-to-please exes? Or a professional?'

CHAPTER TWO

FOR WHAT FELT like the longest time Abby didn't say anything. Didn't do anything. She couldn't. She was speechless. Stunned into immobility.

So much for explaining why she was really here, as she'd been about to. And so much for thinking that she was muddling through what was a hideously awkward situation reasonably all right.

That assumption had been well and truly shot out of the water because had he *really* just said what she thought he'd said? Implied what she thought he'd implied? Did he really think that she'd been sent to seduce him? In a *professional* capacity? Supplied by his *brother*?

Her mind was blank with shock and she was reeling all over again because OK, so he didn't know who she was—the meetings she'd had had always been with Jake, who was the face of the company while Leo very firmly remained in the background, and from what she understood he'd been away a lot of the time anyway—but *seriously*? Didn't he recognise her name? Hadn't he received any of her emails? And was this really the way his supposedly razor-sharp brain worked?

With her jaw about to hit the floor, Abby quite forgot the purpose of the hand-to-eye combo, which wasn't just to protect his modesty but also to stop her from ogling his body, lowered her hand and stared at him.

And immediately wished she hadn't because prone and passed out he'd been impressive, but sitting upright, radiating energy, tension, and well, sheer *presence*, he practically robbed her of breath, never mind speech.

Not that he was exactly waiting for an answer even if she had been able to provide one. No. Now, to add insult to injury, he appeared to be checking her out, looking her over, slowly, lazily and thoroughly, his gaze sliding from her eyes to her mouth to her breasts and lower, lingering over every available inch of her.

And dammit if her body didn't begin to respond to his scrutiny. To her appal, she could feel it happening. The heat pooling in her stomach. The tingles prickling her skin. The tension winding through her muscles and the beginnings of desire, intoxicating and heady and so inappropriate on so many levels she didn't know who she was more disgusted with, herself or him.

'Well?' he asked, finally raising dark, inscrutable eyes to hers and arching an eyebrow.

'I'm none of the above,' she said tartly, silently adding *you obnoxious jerk* and feeling her estimation of him—which had previously been pretty high given everything he and his brother had achieved—plummet through every one of the thirty floors that lay between them and solid ground.

'No?'

'Absolutely not.'

'Well, whatever you are,' he said flatly, 'you've had a wasted journey because I'm not interested.'

And, wham, there was another insult.

Abby swallowed back a gasp and tried not to recoil at the bolt of—what was that? Disappointment? Couldn't be. Hurt? No way. Outrage? Definitely. That was what it was. She was outraged. Offended. Incensed.

And she'd had enough. Certainly of being on the floor and having him looking down on her with such dry disdain, such ice-cold superiority when he was so totally, so unbelievably in the wrong.

Setting her jaw and trying to formulate a response that

wouldn't cost her her job, she grabbed her clipboard and, holding it to her middle like some sort of a shield, stood up.

'Actually,' she said, fixing a cool smile to her face and just about keeping a lid on the urge to tell him exactly what she thought of him because however much of a jerk he was he was still a client, and an influential one at that, 'I *am* here in a professional capacity, just not the one you're thinking of.'

'Oh?'

'I'm an event organiser,' she said, then added pointedly, '*Your* event organiser. And you're paying me a lot for the privilege, so there's absolutely nothing "gifty" about it at all.'

There followed a couple of seconds of silence as presumably this sank into his seriously warped brain and then something that she hoped might be mortification flickered across his face.

'My event organiser,' he echoed with a faint frown, as if it was taking considerable effort to assimilate the information, which maybe it was because his head was clearly a mess. But, ooh, she didn't like the way he emphasised the 'my', whether he'd meant it that way or not.

'Yours and Jake's,' she clarified, then added in a tone so chilly it could have frozen the Sahara, 'And just in case we're still not clear, the event I've organised for this evening is your Christmas-slash-ten-year-anniversary party taking place right now downstairs. The party you're meant to be at. Thanking your staff for all their hard work this year, celebrating your success, and generally being around looking full of festive cheer.' Instead of being upstairs, unconscious as the result of a drinking spree and then flinging potentially slanderous allegations about the place.

His jaw tightened, his dark eyes narrowed and she thought that she'd never seen anyone less full of festive cheer, but that wasn't her problem.

'What time is it?' he asked.

'Seven.'

He swore and raked his hands through his hair and she kept her eyes firmly on his face, not lowering them to watch the play of muscles and the stretch of his chest caused by the gesture for even a second. 'I overslept,' he muttered with a frown.

If that was the way he wanted to put it, she thought, swallowing hard and locking her knees because she might have peeked just for a moment and she might be feeling a bit faint, then that was up to him. If he thought it all right to drink himself into oblivion and shirk his responsibilities, then fine. 'Apparently so.'

'Long night,' he said with a faint apologetic smile that didn't mollify her in the slightest. 'And an even longer day. On top of some pretty hideous jet lag.'

'None of my business,' she said, as interested in his excuses as much as she was interested in why he hadn't had a woman in his bed for years. Which was absolutely not at all. 'What *is* my business is that dinner's in half an hour and people are wondering where you are, which is why Jake sent me to look for you.'

He nodded and rubbed a hand along his jaw. 'I see.'

'Do you?' she asked a bit archly because there seemed to be an awful lot he hadn't seen in the last ten minutes, such as the clipboard, which surely marked her out as anything other than a lady of the night and to which she was now clinging as if it were a reminder to keep a grip on the self-control that was badly in danger of unravelling. 'Really? Well, that's great. And now I have found you, I'll be going.'

She shot him a quick, professional smile and then turned on her heel because she really had to get out of there before she either said or, worse, did something she'd regret, only to jerk to a halt when he said, 'Wait.'

'What?' she said, swivelling round and seeing his smile deepen and turn into something so unexpected, so lethally attractive, that she went all hot and dizzy and once again forgot that she was anything other than a woman badly in need of kissing.

'I believe I owe you an apology.'

She blinked, totally thrown by the switch in his demeanour and the change to his features, but somehow managed to keep that smile fixed to her face. 'Accepted.'

'I was out of order. Not thinking straight. Half asleep.'

'It's fine,' she said. 'Forget it. I have. Now if you'll excuse me, I ought to be getting back to the party, so I'll tell Jake you'll be down in, what, ten minutes?'

Leo ran a hand through his hair and then grimaced, his smile turning from lethal to wry, although no less devastating for it, and Abby steeled herself against its effect before taking a hasty step back towards the door, towards escape.

'As for some reason I appear to smell like a distillery,' he said dryly, 'you'd better make it twenty.'

Twenty minutes might have been long enough to wash away the foul smell of stale whisky and douse the heat and desire that Abby had unexpectedly conjured up in him, but it wasn't nearly long enough to figure out what the hell had been going on with him back there in his bedroom.

Tugging his cuffs out from beneath the sleeves of his jacket, Leo set his jaw and strode into the lift, the excruciating details of the last half an hour or so slamming into his head all over again.

Had he really accused her of basically being a prostitute? Had he really thought Jake would organise something like that? And had he really not only eyed her up but actually, for the briefest, maddest moment while overwhelmed by inexplicable lust, seriously considered taking her up on an offer that wasn't even on the table?

What was the matter with him?

Feeling strangely short of breath in a way that had nothing to do with the faster-than-lightning descent of the lift,

Leo ran a finger around the inside of his collar to ease it and wished he could wipe the whole mortifying scene from his brain.

There were faintly mitigating circumstances, it was true. His brain had been fogged up with sleep and he'd been disorientated. In something of a state of shock and very confused. And then there was the fact that he was absolutely exhausted as a result of work, travel and the time of the year, which always gave him sleepless nights and set him on edge.

But was any of that an excuse? No, it wasn't. If he'd been thinking clearly he'd have waited for her to explain, would have given her at least the nanosecond of a chance before rushing in with his ridiculous assumptions. He'd have clocked the clipboard earlier and probably come to a very different conclusion.

He'd certainly have kept his mouth shut. Silence was an excellent and effective weapon, he knew that, and if only his brain hadn't been completely addled he wouldn't have dug himself into a hole so deep that, despite her apparent acceptance of his apology, he wasn't sure he'd got out of it.

But then he hadn't been thinking clearly. Or rationally. He hadn't been thinking at all. At least not with his head. For the majority of their encounter he'd been thinking with a different part of his anatomy entirely.

At the image of Abby standing there, beautiful blue eyes flashing while she set him straight, magnificent in her indignation and her efforts to hide it, a wave of heat surged through him, making his pulse spike and, to his frustration, his body harden.

Ruthlessly deleting the image, Leo reminded himself of the ice-cold shower he'd just taken, and as the lift doors opened and he stepped out he decided to delete the rest of the episode up there in his bedroom too, because how the hell was he supposed to get through this evening if he kept remembering how much he'd wanted to take her to bed?

Doing up the button of his dinner jacket, he strode in the direction of the venue for tonight's celebrations, searching for the clarity of thought and steely self-control he'd always taken for granted and just about finding it.

There was nothing he could do to undo what had happened, he reasoned, but with any luck his and Abby's paths wouldn't cross again. She'd be working and he'd be doing the thanking of his staff and attempting—though probably failing—to dispense the festive cheer she'd mentioned. Once the evening was over he'd never have to think of her or his fifteen minutes of complete mental meltdown ever again.

Taking a certain amount of comfort from that, Leo felt the churning in his stomach subside and the mess in his head dissolve, and walked through the double doors that led into the room that was being used to serve drinks and canapés.

Inwardly wincing at the noise level—which had to be ten times anything he'd ever encountered on a building site—he accepted a glass of champagne from the tray of a passing waiter, and set about draining it in the hope it might obliterate the memory of that humiliating half an hour in his bedroom.

'Good of you to make it,' came a dry, amused voice from his left that had him jolting mid-swallow and nearly choking on the champagne.

'Thanks for that,' said Leo, once he'd recovered from both the champagne going down the wrong way and his brother's efforts to rectify the situation, which had involved a lot of back thumping and drink spillage.

'Sorry,' said Jake, not sounding in the slightest bit apologetic. 'So what kept you?'

'Jet lag,' he muttered. 'Knocked me for six.'

'Ah. I did wonder. I thought you might be deliberately avoiding the party.'

'Why would I do that?'

'You hate them.'

That was true, but, 'This isn't a party,' he said. 'This is work.'

'Try telling that to our guests.'

Leo swapped his empty glass for a full one, took a long gulp and forced himself to focus. 'How's it going?' he asked, his gaze drifting over the throngs of people all drinking and eating and full of the Christmas spirit he found so hard to muster up while he identified staff members, clients, architects, planning officers and financiers among the guests, and resolutely did not look for a certain slim, strawberry blonde event organiser.

'Pretty good so far.' Jake helped himself to something that looked like a mini Yorkshire pudding. 'Thanks to Abby,' he added. 'Whom you've met, I gather.'

'I have,' said Leo, annoyed with himself for being tempted to seek her out when she shouldn't even be crossing his mind, and then thinking that actually 'met' wasn't quite the word he'd have used. Insulted. That was probably an appropriate one. Or offended. That would work equally well.

'What did you think of her?'

He thought she was gorgeous. Sexy. Very *very* beddable. 'I didn't think anything of her, particularly,' he said, his voice not betraying a hint of the lie. 'Why?'

Jake wiped his fingers on a napkin and grinned. 'Just wondering.'

'What do *you* think of her?' asked Leo before he could stop himself.

'She's great. Extremely capable. Has a knack for knowing exactly what's needed, a talent for solving problems with the minimum amount of fuss and a rare ability to stick to the budget. Plus, she's single and incredibly hot.'

Leo felt his jaw tighten for a second but channelled nonchalance he really didn't feel and said, as if he couldn't give a toss, 'Is she? I hadn't noticed.' Which was another lie because like hell he hadn't.

Jake grinned. 'No, well, you wouldn't, would you? A

dozen naked women could parade right in front of you and you'd be oblivious.'

'I prefer subtlety.'

'As I don't, I might ask her for a dance later.'

'Go for it,' said Leo, just about managing not to grit his teeth.

'Although I wouldn't be entirely surprised if she said no.'

'Why?'

When Jake didn't immediately answer, Leo glanced over to find his brother looking at him questioningly. 'What the hell happened up there?'

Hmm.

Leo picked up a tiny blini topped with sour cream and caviar and ate it slowly, largely to give himself time to work out how he was going to respond, because wasn't that the question of the night? And one to which there was no answer, because for one thing he still hadn't entirely worked it out, and for another, hell would freeze over before he shared the details of the misunderstanding that made him look like such a complete and utter fool with anyone, least of all his no-holds-barred brother.

'What do you mean, what happened up there?' he said evenly, deciding that bluffing was the only way through this. 'Nothing happened up there.'

'Right,' said Jake, clearly not believing him for a second. 'Then why did Abby come down looking like thunder?'

Leo shrugged and kept his eyes on the party. 'No idea,' he said and took another gulp of champagne.

'What did you do?'

'Why would you think I did anything?'

'It's that time of year. Makes you morose. Edgy. Unpredictable. But more than that, she was fine when I asked her to go up and find you.'

'Maybe she had a call. Maybe something's gone wrong with the catering. Who knows?'

There was a pause and Leo glanced at Jake to find him looking back shrewdly. 'I think I might have some idea.'

Leo went still, his fingers tightening around the stem of his glass as his pulse sped up. Had Abby said something? Given Jake a minute-by-minute account of what had happened? And were there perhaps ramifications to what he'd done? Hadn't people been sued for less?

'Really?' he said, hedging his bets but bracing himself for the worst.

Jake nodded. 'Yup. She's a perfectionist. She doesn't like things to go wrong.'

'No, well, what event planner would?'

'So perhaps finding you passed out after a drinking session piqued her sense of responsibility and orderliness.'

Leo frowned and wondered if his brain was still on go-slow because what on earth was Jake on about? What drinking session? 'Passed out?' he echoed.

'That was her guess.'

'It was the wrong one.'

'You should have mentioned the jet lag,' said Jake dryly. 'Then she might have been a little less disapproving.'

'I doubt it,' said Leo, wishing that his state of sobriety had been the only misunderstanding of the night.

'Why, what else happened?' said Jake, and Leo mentally kicked himself for forgetting that while his brother sometimes came across as being so laid-back he was horizontal, he also had a sky-high IQ and an irritating talent for zooming in on things that one might prefer to be glossed over.

'There may have been a slight misunderstanding,' he said, resigning himself to the knowledge that he was going to have to divulge at least something of the events of half an hour ago because Jake could be surprisingly tenacious when the mood took him.

'What kind of misunderstanding?'

'Nothing important, and it was cleared up.'

'Did it involve me?'

'Why would you think it involved you?'

'Because when she was telling me you were on your way down she kept giving me the filthiest looks. It made me want to ditch the champagne and break into the bottle of single malt I was planning on giving to you.'

Leo went still. 'Single malt?'

'To drown your woes and cheer you up. The present I was talking about to get you through Christmas.'

'That was the present?'

'Of course. What else would I have meant?'

What else indeed? Damn. He really had got things wrong. Badly *badly* wrong.

'Are you all right?'

Leo snapped back to find his brother watching him closely. 'Why wouldn't I be?'

'You've gone pale and you're frowning.'

'I'm fine.' Or he would be once he'd come to terms with the realisation that for the first time in years he'd abandoned logic, reason and self-control, and had basically totally lost his mind.

What the hell was wrong with him this evening? he wondered for what felt like the hundredth time. Was it really merely jet lag and the time of year? Or was he coming down with something? Something he'd picked up on his travels maybe?

More to the point, why was Jake looking at him like that?

'Oh, my God,' said his brother, his jaw dropping as his expression turned to one of disbelief. 'You didn't.'

'I didn't what?'

'Think *Abby* was the present.'

'Of course not,' said Leo with a short laugh that didn't sound as dismissive as he'd intended.

'You did.'

'Don't be absurd.'

'I'm not the one being absurd. You did. You really did. And you claim to prefer subtlety.'

As this was a conversation he really didn't want to be having Leo ran a hand along his jaw, shifted his attention to the party going on in front of them and, in a probably pointless effort at distraction, said, 'Did I mention how great this place looks? Excellent tree.'

'Forget the decorations,' said Jake, sounding astounded, incredulous and appalled. 'How on earth could you think I'd ever do something like that?'

Leo arched an eyebrow and swung his gaze back to his brother. 'Well, it wouldn't be the first time, would it?'

Jake looked as stunned as if he'd thumped him in the stomach. 'What?'

'Remember the stripper?'

'That was twelve years ago,' said his brother, after a moment. 'For a mate for his eighteenth birthday, and he'd specifically requested it. Don't you think I might have matured a bit since then?' He ran his hands through his hair and then shook his head in disbelief. 'Jeez,' he said, blowing out a breath. 'Thanks for that. I think I might be seriously offended.'

'I think Abby might have been too.'

There was another stunned silence as Jake stared at him apparently briefly lost for words. 'You *confronted* her with it?'

Leo shrugged, keeping the cringing very firmly on the inside. 'I wasn't thinking straight. Half asleep, in fact. Disorientated. Like I said, jet lag.'

'Not an excuse.'

'I know.'

'How did she take it?'

'How do you think?'

Jake, who wasn't nearly as good as Leo at containing his emotions, winced. 'Did you apologise?'

'Yes.'

'And explain?'

'I didn't get the chance. She didn't stick around.'

Now he thought about it, he hadn't had a woman flee from him quite so fast since the excruciating afternoon exactly five years ago when Lisa had raced back down the aisle the wrong way, leaving him standing, jilted, at the altar. But he could hardly blame Abby. He'd probably been lucky to get away without a slap to the face.

'I'm not surprised,' said Jake.

'Neither am I.'

There was a moment's silence during which Jake, presumably struggling to come to terms with what had happened, gave his head a couple more shakes in disbelief. Then he sobered, fixed Leo with a look that spoke volumes and said, 'So do you think it's going to be a problem?'

'Not if I can help it,' said Leo darkly as a pair of doors swung open and dinner was announced.

CHAPTER THREE

FOR SOMEONE WHO didn't merit a moment's thought, Leo was remarkably difficult to ignore.

It wasn't as if Abby had had time to daydream about him or what had happened up there in his apartment. She'd had more than enough to keep her occupied: timings to keep track of; a supper of turkey with all the trimmings followed by Christmas-pudding-flavoured ice cream to get out; the blowing of the lights on the tree that had required a couple of tricky bulb replacements; a DJ who'd spent half an hour grumbling about the inadequate positioning of his speakers and had taken ten minutes to mollify.

Yet even though their paths hadn't crossed, if someone asked her where he was she'd be able to tell them.

Right now, for example, she was taking a moment to watch the heaving dance floor, and she didn't need to look around to know that he was lounging at a table on the far side of the room, nursing a glass of whisky and looking as if he'd rather be anywhere than here, despite being the sole focus of an attractive brunette.

It was strange. And baffling, because yes, at well over six feet tall he stood head and shoulders above almost everyone, and yes, he had that presence that had had such a troubling effect on her when she'd been within a couple of feet of him, but so what? She'd met many tall, imposing men in her line of work and she'd never had a problem with not thinking about *them*.

But with Leo it was as if she were a satnav and he were her destination. When she was out of his orbit she felt oddly disorientated and a bit lost, and when she did spot him she instantly felt compelled to make her way over to him.

The awareness was weird. Confusing. And for someone who liked to be in control of the situation at all times, not a little disconcerting. All the more so because fancying a man who was a deplorable jerk—no matter how good-looking he was—was simply downright perverse.

But that was another thing that had been perplexing her as the evening had ticked along. If he was so tactlessly awful, wouldn't people have been avoiding him all night? There would have been a sycophantic few, of course, but this was a party where the guests were out to enjoy themselves and she'd have thought the majority would have steered well clear.

Yet all night he'd been surrounded. She'd seen him smiling and chatting, albeit with a faintly cool, aloof air about him, and there was no doubt that people seemed to actually like him. They'd sought him out, and then hung around. Especially the women. They still were, even now, when everything about him indicated he'd rather be left alone.

All of which made her think that while she was pretty sure she hadn't misheard or misinterpreted his words or the outrageous way he'd checked her out, maybe he wasn't the man she'd assumed him to be, and therefore perhaps she was as guilty of leaping to the wrong conclusion as he was.

Maybe he was just one of those people who took a while to wake up properly and had been a bit disorientated. Maybe there was some kind of explanation for what had happened and maybe she should have stuck around and asked for it instead of overreacting and fleeing the scene as if the hounds of hell were at her heels.

Not that it mattered. Maybes were all very well but the time for clarification was long gone. And she could find him as devastatingly attractive as she liked but nothing would ever come of it, would it?

The guy was way out of her league, and, even if he weren't, even if he weren't a client, he'd made it spectacularly clear that he wasn't interested in her, so there was no point secretly wondering what might have happened if she'd thrown caution to the wind and actually kissed him when she had the chance. No point at all, and it was therefore annoying in the extreme that the idea of it had been—and still was—buzzing around her head like some kind of manic bee.

Abby rubbed at her temples as if that might somehow miraculously make the thought go away, but it didn't. Perhaps actually getting on with the long list of things that still needed doing instead of dreamily and wistfully watching the dance floor, and very definitely not Leo, would.

Pulling herself together and focusing on that mental list, she spun on her heel. And went slap bang into a tall male figure.

'Oof,' she mumbled as she recoiled off a hard chest, and a pair of hands gripped her shoulders.

'Steady on.'

Taking a moment to catch her breath as the hands released her, she stepped back and looked up into the face of Jake. And dammit if she wasn't somehow *disappointed*.

Dismissing that as completely nuts, instead Abby ran a quick check of her heart rate and her body temperature, and briefly marvelled at how Jake, in contrast to his brother, should have so little effect on her when he was just as imposing and just as good-looking. Although he did lack the dark, brooding—and apparently irresistible—thing Leo had going on.

'Sorry,' she said with a smart professional smile and a quick mental reminder that she wasn't to think about Leo any further.

'No problem.'

'I was just heading to the kitchens.'

'And I was just coming to see if you wanted to dance.'

Abby blinked. 'Dance?' she echoed, faintly taken aback because she couldn't think of a time when the line between being an employee and a guest had ever blurred before.

'Yeah,' said Jake with a grin. 'You know, that thing where you shuffle your feet around and move, generally in time to music.'

His smile was contagious and she had to force herself not to automatically reciprocate it because, despite all the great things she'd thought he was, he was also very possibly a man who procured 'fun' for his brother. 'Thank you,' she said politely, 'but I'm working.'

Jake rocked on his heels and studied her. 'I heard about what happened earlier.'

Abby instinctively tensed but she continued to look up at him calmly. 'Did you?'

'You do realise that it had nothing to do with me, don't you?'

'Didn't it?'

'Of course not.'

'Then what did it have to do with?'

Jake grinned and shrugged. 'I have absolutely no idea. It's generally impossible to work out what's going on in the head of that brother of mine. I'm not nearly as complicated.'

'No?'

'No. And I'm certainly not interested in getting involved with his sex life.' He shuddered theatrically, then looked at her assessingly for a while, as if weighing up his chances and then coming to the conclusion it was worth a gamble. 'So how about that dance?'

And this time Abby couldn't help smiling back, because, if she was being honest, she'd never really been able to reconcile the Jake she'd come to know over the weeks with the man she'd briefly considered he might be. It hadn't made any sense, hadn't seemed right.

'I'd love to,' she said, now with genuine regret because

she enjoyed dancing, 'but I really can't. There are so many things that still need to be done.'

'Come on,' said Jake cajolingly. 'It's Christmas. You and your team have done an amazing job tonight. Surely you can relax for five minutes. You deserve it. Besides, you know you want to.'

'How do you figure that?'

'You were swaying and your feet were tapping so hard I was beginning to fear for my carpet.'

He was right, and as the music segued into an irresistible mash-up of Christmas tunes she could feel it happening again. Her feet were itching and her body was tingling with the urge to move. And whether it was the effect of his charm and powers of persuasion or the sudden overwhelming need to burn off her frustration at her totally wrecked peace of mind she didn't know. All she knew was that she was going to relent.

'All right,' she said and instantly felt the pressure inside her ease, 'I guess five minutes wouldn't hurt.'

'Great,' said Jake, taking her hand and leading her towards the dance floor. 'Let's hit it.'

Ten seconds ago Leo had been semi-engaged in a one-sided conversation with a planning officer for an East London council and thinking about heading upstairs to bed because he'd had more than enough of tonight.

Firstly he'd hit his limit with all this relentless festive bloody cheer about an hour ago, and if he had to agree one more time that, yes, Christmas was a lovely time of year when frankly he couldn't think of a less lovely time of year he wouldn't be responsible for the consequences. And secondly he was sick to the back teeth of the unusual, unnerving and deeply unwelcome way that tonight he hadn't been able to concentrate on, well, *anything*, really.

All he wanted, therefore, was to leave, find some space and some distance to sort himself out.

However the moment he spied his brother first leading Abby onto the dance floor and then taking her into his arms, semi-engagement in the conversation turned to disengagement, his mood turned from bad to filthy and any intention he might have had of going vanished.

Oh, dammit all to hell. Just when he thought he'd got over his ridiculous fixation with Abby, there she was, right in front of him, derailing his thoughts and destroying his concentration.

All night he'd been aware of her, flitting in and out of the room while she presumably checked that everything was on track and kept Jake up to speed with what was going on. Every time he caught a glimpse of reddish-blonde hair he'd found his attention veering away from whatever conversation he was having in case it was her, which, nine times out of ten, it wasn't.

This time, however, it was, although what she was doing on the dance floor and in Jake's arms he had no idea.

Or did he? Hadn't Jake mentioned he'd be asking her to dance? And hadn't he, Leo, told him to go for it? He had, and given how persuasive he knew Jake could be he shouldn't be surprised that Abby had fallen for it. It wasn't his concern *who* she danced with, so that thing burning inside him wasn't jealousy, of course, because that would be absurd. No, it was boiling frustration that he hadn't been able to get her out of his mind, that he was somehow *off* tonight, and that once a-bloody-gain the conversation he'd been sort of having was history, that was all.

'Leo?' said the woman beside him, and with annoying difficulty he snapped his attention away from the dance floor to his companion.

At least he could be sure that his expression reflected none of the mess churning around inside him, he thought, giving her a quick smile as if that might make up for the fact he didn't have a clue what she'd been saying. 'What?'

'What do you think?'

'Let's talk next week,' he said, going for non-committal and generic in the hope that it covered all bases, which apparently it did.

'I'll call you.'

'Great,' he said, his attention already fading and his gaze involuntarily sliding back to the dance floor, more specifically to the woman in the middle of it who was now beginning to move.

'Would you like to dance?'

'I'm afraid I don't.'

'I see,' said Anna? Hannah? Susanna? with a faint smile. 'You're the type that likes to watch.'

And it seemed he was, because despite his best efforts to the contrary he couldn't take his eyes off Abby. At first she seemed to be messing around, dancing as cheesily as the music, but then something slower came on and her moves gentled, became less frenetic, more languid, more sinuous. Jake twirled her and dipped her, tried—and alarmingly pleasingly failed—to pull her in close, and the longer he watched, the more transfixed Leo became.

It was odd, he thought, his pulse beating unnaturally fast. It wasn't as if she were the most beautiful woman he'd ever met, so why was he so aware of her? Why did he find her so arresting? So compelling? Why did he want to leap to his feet, shove Jake aside and take over?

None of it made any sense, and because it didn't he didn't like it one little bit. It meant he didn't know what was happening and therefore wasn't in control, which was a situation he hadn't experienced for years and had taken great care to avoid.

But Abby was a situation he couldn't avoid because unfortunately, later, he was going to have to seek her out.

When Jake had asked him before dinner if what had happened up there in his flat was going to be a problem he hadn't needed to expand. They were both well aware that their reputation was a fragile thing. Not all their developments were popular and their opponents would use anything they could lay their hands on to influence planning decisions. As his brother was always saying, the integrity of the company—and the two of them—was of utmost importance, and if anything called it into question serious damage could be done.

And while Leo might be the numbers man who preferred to stay in the background and leave all the publicity stuff to his brother, the business and its success meant everything to him. He hadn't spent years building it up only to have it potentially destroyed by one moment of lunacy, so if Abby had a problem with what had happened earlier he'd fix it. The sooner the better. He really had no choice.

To that end, he ought to be figuring out a strategy, not watching his brother maul Abby and grinding his teeth. Somewhere else, because here he was barely able to think straight, let alone strategise, so, with a muttered excuse and a tight smile to the planning officer whose name he couldn't remember, Leo got to his feet.

He shot Abby one last quick glance, which was a mistake because for one split second she returned it, and he nearly crashed into a table. Taking the feeling that he'd been thumped in the solar plexus and then bashed over the head as pretty much par for the course this evening, Leo set his jaw and made for the exit.

Alone in the vast conference room that had doubled up as the venue for tonight's celebrations, Abby flopped onto a chair, eased her heels off with a grimace and flexed her toes. God, that felt good. Her shoes were about as comfortable as shoes could get, but after six hours on her feet and then a quarter of an hour on that dance floor she could quite happily do with never setting eyes on the damn things ever again.

Crossing one leg over the other and massaging one of her soles, she glanced round the dimly lit room, now cleared of the festive decorations that had festooned the place, the crockery, the cutlery, the glassware and the tablecloths, and, in contrast to the noisy buzz of earlier, eerily silent.

Tomorrow the tables would go, the dance floor would be dismantled and the room once again divided into three, but just for five minutes, before she turned off the one remaining light and left, she could reminisce and indulge in the satisfaction of a job well done.

All in all, tonight had been quite a night, she thought with a smile as her mind drifted over the events of the evening. The food, the drink and the entertainment had all gone off with the minimum of hitches, the guests had had a great time and Jake had been pleased. As far as she knew no one had photocopied their bottom and the stationery cupboard hadn't been commandeered for inappropriate usage.

Of course, with the attention to detail and the meticulous planning she always lavished on every event she organised, she'd have expected nothing less than perfection, and the subcontractors she worked with, most of whom she'd known for years and were the best, knew that. But still. Tonight had been good.

Which was particularly pleasing because this was the first event she'd organised for the Cartwright brothers and she was hoping it wouldn't be the last. Clients like these—who were big, influential, and willing to give her the perfect combination of a generous budget, few requirements and total control—weren't all that common and she wouldn't mind hanging onto them.

She certainly hadn't minded hanging onto Jake when she'd locked gazes with Leo back there on the dance floor and her knees had practically given way, she thought as the giant glitter ball moved a fraction, caught the light and took her back to the moment in question.

It hadn't been so much the look on his face that had rocked her, because that had been as neutral as ever, but it was the sensation that he'd been watching her. Intently. And for a while. That had made her feel all weirdly flustered inside and if Jake hadn't been there to catch her when she stumbled she'd have ignominiously hit the deck.

Leo had disappeared by the time they'd come off the dance floor, thank goodness. So had the brunette, although she didn't want to think about *that* particular coincidence. Switching into work mode a lot later than she should have done, Abby had legged it to the kitchens and from then on had focused on what she was there to do.

She hadn't seen Leo again, and it occurred to her now that the prospect of doing so in the future was highly unlikely. The night was over and even if she did get more work here she'd likely liaise with the relevant department. The only reason she'd had direct contact with Jake about this evening was because he held the admirable and rare view that if he handled things—even if it simply meant hiring her—then it was a party for everyone, not everyone bar the person who had to organise it.

And it was totally fine. Better that way, actually, because Leo Cartwright, whether in her league or out of it, had made her feel all kinds of things she'd really rather not, none of them remotely professional. Plus, he made her think with her body instead of her head, and that was unusual enough to be deeply unsettling, so all in all if she never saw him again, it would be for the best. In fact—

'Here you are.'

At the sound of the deep voice behind her Abby gasped and jumped, and swivelled round to find the man himself standing in the doorway, leaning one shoulder against the frame, his hands in his pockets, his eyes dark and his expression inscrutable as he looked down at her.

She blinked, just in case tiredness had caught up with her and she'd started hallucinating, but no. He was still there. Looking tired and dishevelled with his bow tie hanging untied around his neck and the top couple of buttons of his shirt undone, but nevertheless so devastatingly handsome that she went all hot and tingly while her stomach did a weird kind of swoop.

'Goodness, you gave me a fright,' she said, clapping a hand to her chest as if that might sort out her suddenly erratic breathing.

'Sorry,' he said with the hint of a smile that sent her stomach into free fall all over again, her head into a spin and made her wonder dizzily what it was about him in particular that had her responding so viscerally. 'Although fair's fair, don't you think?'

'Is it?' she said, for a moment not having a clue what he was referring to because all she could think of was how there wasn't anything fair about him at all. Everything was dark. Smoulderingly, broodingly and sizzlingly attractively dark.

'I think so.' A pause. 'Although, strictly speaking, you'd have to be the one who was naked.'

Abby snapped her gaze back to his, to find him watching her with a look of cool amusement on his face. Naked? What on earth was he talking about? Did he want her naked? For a moment yet more heat rushed through her and her heart galloped and she seriously considered leaping off the chair and throwing herself at him.

But then—thank heavens—sanity struck and it suddenly hit her. The penthouse. His state of undress. The misunderstanding. The half an hour she'd been so badly trying to forget.

Really not wanting to go there, Abby hmmed while her heart rate slowed and her body temperature cooled, and decided it might be safer for her poor overworked organs if she changed the subject.

'So what can I do for you?' she asked, trying not to worry because the party had ended an hour ago and why he'd be roaming the ground floor of the hotel at nearly one in the morning she couldn't imagine. 'Is there a problem?'

He shook his head. 'No problem.'

'Then what is it?'

'I wanted to thank you for everything you did this evening.'

A warm glow of professional satisfaction spread through her, momentarily dampening the desire. 'You're welcome.'

'It was a great party.'

'It had good hosts.' She shot him a quick smile. 'Not to mention an excellent planner.'

'The latter is certainly true.'

'Thank you.'

And then that seemed to be that for conversation because Leo didn't say anything else, just carried on looking at her, and quite suddenly Abby found that she couldn't have said anything even if she'd wanted to because their gazes had locked and all she could concentrate on were his eyes. His mesmerising, thought-destroying, soul-shattering eyes…

Dark and bottomless, they were the kind of eyes a girl could lose herself in, she thought dizzily. Totally lose herself in, forgetting everything while clinging to those shoulders and wrapping her legs around his waist and crying out as he smoothly slid inside her, moving slowly at first, then faster and harder, until there were no words, no thoughts, nothing but spiralling tension and breathy moans and then lovely, lovely release…

'Thanking you wasn't the only reason I came to find you,' he said, his words—oddly loud and hoarse in the heavy, thick silence—cutting through her thoughts and making her land back on Earth with a bump.

'Oh?' she said, her voice a lot breathier and her heart beating a lot faster than was appropriate for a woman who never lost herself or clung, and who'd sworn never again to think about what she'd seen when that bed sheet had slipped.

'I'd like to apologise for what happened earlier.'

'You already did,' she said with an overly bright smile, as if beaming like a maniac might somehow detract from the giveaway blush she could feel burning her cheeks and the breathlessness.

'Not enough. Not nearly enough. I was totally out of order.'

'Perhaps.'

'It was a misunderstanding.'

Taking a couple of deep steadying breaths and pulling herself together because she had absolutely no business fantasising about him, Abby twisted round and slipped her feet back into the vices that were her shoes. 'I'll say.'

'But not one I'd ever make under normal circumstances.'

'No, well, I guess the circumstances weren't all that normal,' she said, trying not to wince as leather heel met sore blister.

'They weren't. I've spent the last month scoping out development possibilities across a dozen countries on three continents. I barely know what time zone I'm in.'

'As you said, I must have given you quite a shock.'

He nodded. 'You did.'

'You were probably a bit disorientated. Confused, even.'

'I was. And I'm sorry.'

'It's fine,' she said with a wave of her hand and a reassuring smile as she straightened and turned back to him. 'Really. It's not an issue.'

'Are you sure?'

She nodded, crossed her legs to ease at least one of her poor lacerated heels and linked her hands around her knee. 'Absolutely. I'm not going to go round telling everyone you

accused me of being a prostitute, if that's what
ried about.'

He arched an eyebrow. 'No?'

'Of course not. In my business discretion is a given.
Whatever the occasion and whatever the circumstances. So
your secret is perfectly safe with me.'

His expression didn't flicker for a second, but Abby
thought she detected a slight ease in the tension gripping
his shoulders and there was definitely a faint smile playing
at his mouth. 'Thank you.'

'Anyway, I'm sure there are perfectly valid reasons for
thinking that your brother would procure a prostitute for
you,' she said, curiosity getting the better of her because
the Cartwright brothers were notoriously private, this one
being especially hard to read, and she suddenly wanted to
know *everything*.

'Possibly.'

'Care to share them?'

'Not particularly.' He rubbed a hand along his jaw and
regarded her thoughtfully. 'You know, I'd actually quite like
to forget about the whole thing.'

'Oh, so would I, so would I,' she said with a regretful
shake of her head as she decided she wasn't above a little
emotional manipulation if it meant finding out what was
going on behind that stony façade of his. 'But you see it's
going to niggle away at me for *days*.' She bit her lip and
frowned. 'And now I think about it, maybe I do deserve an
explanation.'

Leo arched an eyebrow. 'In return for your silence?'

She tsked and grinned. 'You make it sound like blackmail.'

'Isn't it?'

'Not at all. It's a simple clarification of the facts for the
purposes of moving forward.'

He tilted his head, his smile deepening a little. 'Fair
enough. Jet lag doesn't suit me.'

'I wouldn't have thought excessive alcohol suited jet lag.'

'It doesn't.'

'Then why the overindulgence?'

'I wouldn't call an inch of whisky an overindulgence.'

'An inch?'

He nodded. 'An inch.'

'You could have fooled me,' said Abby dryly. 'The place reeked.'

'I know. And I also know why.'

'Now I'm intrigued.'

'Exhaustion caught up with me while I was at my desk. I crashed out. I must have knocked over the glass. Got the stuff all over me.'

The glass on its side and the stained papers in his study flashed into her head and Abby nodded. 'That sounds feasible, I suppose. And Jake's part in the proceedings? Because to be honest he doesn't seem like the procuring type.'

'He isn't. What he offered to send me was actually a bottle of malt.'

'Ah,' she said slowly, as it all became clear. 'And therein lies the misunderstanding.'

'Quite.'

'Embarrassing.'

'Not my finest moment,' he said dryly.

'I can imagine.' She nodded, then as the going had been pretty good so far decided to push a little further. 'So why do you need cheering up?'

'It's been a long week,' he said without even a flicker of hesitation.

'We all have those,' she said. 'Doesn't always lead to a misunderstanding like that.'

'No.'

'So?' she said, wondering firstly when she'd last had a conversation that was quite such hard work, and secondly why she wasn't just giving up on it.

'I'm not a huge fan of Christmas.'

Abby stared at him. Crikey, who didn't like Christmas? 'Really?' she asked. 'Why not? I love it.' Not least because it was excellent for her bank balance.

'I find it...' He paused, as if searching for the right description. 'Uncomfortable.'

'Uncomfortable?' That was an odd word to use.

'Everything closes down, you can't get anything done, it goes on for far too long and the quest for Christmas spirit is relentless. It's over the top, tacky, not to mention a load of commercial crap.'

'Oh,' said Abby, faintly taken aback by the extent of his list of Christmas grievances—most of which were her reasons for liking it—although it certainly explained the way he'd seemed so distant during the party. 'Well, that would do it.'

He nodded briefly. 'Good. So there you go. Not a fan of Christmas.'

'Evidently not.'

'I'm not a huge fan of dancing either, but you are. You do it well, by the way. Very well.'

Leo hadn't moved but something about his mood had changed. Darkened a bit. Made her shiver, although definitely not with cold. 'I'm surprised you noticed,' she said, her voice a note lower than normal. 'You seemed rather engrossed in conversation.'

'Oh, I noticed,' he said softly. 'And you noticed I noticed.'

Damn, had he seen her stumble? Had he worked out why? How deeply humiliating if he had.

Deciding that was a direction in which she really didn't want the conversation to go, Abby made a point of peering round him. 'What happened to the brunette?' she asked, aiming for mere curiosity, not jealousy, and just about managing it.

'I have no idea. What happened to Jake?'

'I don't know.'

Silence fell again, tense and crackling, and as she looked at everything but him her mind raced with questions such as why had Leo suddenly brought that particular moment up? *Why?* And what was she supposed to do with it?

Nothing, was the answer to that, she thought, and when she couldn't stand the awful silence any longer she glanced at her watch and grimaced because, oh, great, she had to be up in five hours.

'Well,' she said, shooting him a quick glance and an overly bright smile. 'You might not be a fan of Christmas but I'm not a fan of two a.m., so I should be heading home.'

Frowning slightly, Leo pushed himself off the door frame. 'Of course,' he said, running his hands through his hair, dishevelling it a bit more. 'Can I call you a taxi?'

'I have my car just outside.'

'Then I'll walk you to it.'

And even though he made her feel nervy and on edge, to say nothing of what he did to her internal organs, as it was late and undoubtedly dark and deserted on the street and she wasn't an idiot, Abby nodded and smiled, and said, 'That would be kind. Thank you.'

CHAPTER FOUR

WHATEVER IT WAS that he was feeling, thought Leo, watching Abby get to her feet with a faint wince, and striding forwards to pick up her coat from the chair it was currently draped over, it wasn't kind.

Part of him felt relief. In contrast to the last time they'd spoken the conversation they'd just had had gone better than he'd expected. He might have spent the last hour or so pacing around the lobby of the hotel driving himself nuts with thoughts of how difficult she could make things for them if she wanted, while he waited for her to finish so he could catch her alone, but thankfully there hadn't been a problem.

He needn't have worried because conversationally he'd actually got off very lightly indeed. Apologising again had been a breeze. Explaining had only been mildly uncomfortable. And he hadn't even had to go into too much detail about why this time of year always set him on edge because to his surprise—and relief—Abby had bought his pretty flimsy excuses.

Physically, though, well, that was an entirely different story because he hadn't got off lightly at all. He'd thought he'd had it tough when he'd been watching her dancing earlier and had been filled with the ridiculous urge to shove Jake aside and take over. He'd thought feeling winded and dazed after just a look had been bad enough.

But that had been nothing compared to what had happened around five minutes ago when their eyes had met and held and held and held.

That had been downright freaky because on contact, time

had seemed to stand absolutely still. He'd felt his entire body jolt and he could have sworn the ground rocked beneath his feet. His mouth had gone dry, his pulse had gone into overdrive and his head had spun.

Feeling totally adrift mentally as well as physically, he'd racked his brains for something to say—anything to break the increasingly tension-laden silence—but all he'd been able to think was that he wanted her, desperately, inexplicably, and he'd been pretty sure that if he'd opened his mouth that was what would have come out.

Thank goodness he'd come to his senses in the nick of time. If he hadn't, if he'd told her all the things he wanted to do to her, she'd have been onto the police within seconds. And he might have put on a convincing front as he'd answered her questions and plied her with excuses, but it had taken practically every drop of self-control that he had not to say to hell with it, march over there and just kiss her.

It was why he'd stayed where he was jammed against the door frame instead of perhaps taking the seat next to her, and it was why it was a good idea she left now. His mood was fragile and his behaviour clearly volatile and the last thing he needed was the slap in the face he might have deserved earlier.

So he'd put her in her coat, see her to her car, and that would be that. He'd slam her door shut, watch her drive off, and put the whole uncomfortable night behind him. And then order would be restored and he could work on getting himself back to normal.

Feeling calmer than he had done in hours now that he had a plan and the end was in sight, Leo held out her coat and tried to defend himself against the effect of her. Five more minutes of this madness. That was all he had to endure. Surely he could hang on that long.

But apparently he couldn't because she flashed him a quick smile that made him look at her mouth, then turned and slipped first one arm and then the other through the sleeves and Leo found himself responding, quite helpless to do anything about it.

He wanted to put his hands on her shoulders and turn her around. He wanted to pull her right up against him and kiss the life out of her, then back her up against the wall and do a whole lot more than kissing. Or drag her with him to the floor or lift her onto a table. He wasn't fussy.

It was her mouth, he thought, his head swimming with the unfamiliar intensity of his reaction to her. Red with lipstick, wide and full, and, well, the only word he could think of was *luscious*, which although not a word he could say he'd ever used before was somehow the only one that would do.

Or her scent. Something about it was intoxicating him, making a total mess of his control and scrambling his brain but also triggering something buried in there deep. A memory, a feeling, a sensation, perhaps...

'Thank you,' she said, taking a step forwards, away from him, then turning and smiling up at him again as she started to do up her buttons.

'Flowers,' he muttered, shoving his hands through his hair as he struggled to work out what it was because for some reason it seemed important.

'What?' she said, stopping for a moment and lifting her eyebrows in surprise as she glanced up at him.

'Irises. Your scent.'

'What about it?'

'It's familiar.'

'I'm sure I'm not the only one who wears it,' she said, giving him a look that seemed to question his sanity.

'It's more familiar than that.'

He tried to place it. Felt it dangling there, tantalisingly just out of reach. He scoured his brain and racked his memory—

And then it hit him.

The dream. The woman leaning over him, murmuring

his name, touching him, the heat of her body, the warmth of her breath. On his skin, his lips. Close. Very close. In fact too close to suggest anything other than an imminent kiss. From her. From Abby.

Oh, yes, now it was all flooding back.

And quite suddenly, totally unexpectedly, the unbearable tension twisting his muscles snapped and Leo felt like laughing.

The cheek of the woman. The bloody *cheek*. All that talk about discretion and the implicit questioning of his integrity, delivered with such an air of superiority from up there on the moral high ground, and yet if anything *she* ought to be the one asking for *his* discretion and apologising for the near lapse in *her* integrity. Because if he wasn't mistaken— and this time he didn't think he was—she'd been about to kiss him. While he'd been asleep. And if that didn't smack of lack of judgement, lack of professionalism, he didn't know what did.

She'd so nearly got away with it, and he'd bet everything he had that she thought she still had, but she was wrong. Very wrong, because there was no way he was letting this go. Absolutely no way.

And just like that, Leo felt better than he had all night, all week, maybe even all month. He felt more awake, more alert, more alive because this was going to be fun, and as fun was something he hadn't had in a long, long time he was going to savour every single second.

And as all kinds of new and tempting possibilities streaked through his head, he thought with almost dizzying relief that for the first time since he and Abby had met he was back on form, ahead of the game and one hundred per cent back in control.

Her scent was a bit of an odd thing for a man like Leo to fixate on, Abby would have thought, but if that was what floated his boat, that was fine with her. She just wanted to get home, give her body some much-needed respite from everything it had undergone this evening, and put the night behind her.

'Before we go,' he said mildly, 'there's something I'd like to know.'

Abby glanced up and something about the way he was looking at her had every instinct she had leaping to attention.

Uh-oh.

What was going on now? Because the words were spoken casually enough but she didn't like the look of that smile. Or his stance. At all.

His expression, his eyes, were still unreadable but something about him seemed to have changed. He radiated a kind of energy that she hadn't noticed before, a sense of tight control, and she got the spine-tingling impression that he'd become…well, not *predatory*, exactly, but there was no doubt that he was training every drop of his attention on her, planning, and sort of *waiting,* although she couldn't imagine what for.

'What is it?' she said cautiously, not at all sure she wanted to know.

He dug his hands into the pockets of his trousers and fixed her with a look that for some reason made her want to squirm. 'What happened between you coming into my bedroom and me waking up?'

Oh. For a nanosecond Abby went still, but then she forced herself to relax, cut the eye contact and continue with her buttons because there was absolutely no way he could know. No. Way.

'What do you mean, what happened?' she muttered, frowning and biting her lip in the hope that she looked as if she didn't have a clue what he was talking about. 'Nothing happened.'

'Talk me through it,' he said lazily. 'Humour me.'

'Couldn't I humour you on Monday?' she said, flashing him a quick, cool smile. 'It's late and I've had a long day.'

'Surely it shouldn't take too long.'

Deciding that if she carried on protesting he'd think—rightly—that she had something to hide, Abby looked at him for a second and then narrowed her eyes as if trying to remember. 'OK, fine,' she said, tapping her forefinger against her mouth and focusing on a spot somewhere high above his right shoulder. 'Now, let me think. Ah, yes. I knocked. There was no answer so I went in. Saw you lying there and gave you a prod then a shake, upon which you woke up.'

'You didn't need to be on your knees to do that.'

'I thought something might have happened to you. Something bad, perhaps fatal. Silly, I suppose,' she said, going a bit red because with hindsight it had been, 'but what with the alcohol, I wanted to check you were OK.'

He nodded, his eyes glinting in the dim light. 'I see. And then?'

'I told you. I poked you and then you woke up.'

'Just like that?'

'After a bit of an effort on my part. I had to shake you hard.'

'So why did you need to lean in so close?'

She froze, her mouth going dry. Did he know? No, he couldn't. 'I didn't.' She frowned, as if running over the scene for the first time all evening, as if it weren't etched probably permanently into her memory. 'Well, I suppose I may have leaned in a *bit*,' she amended, wondering how far 'a bit' could stretch. 'Just to check your breathing and your pulse, but I wouldn't call it *close*.'

'And you didn't whisper my name?'

'Absolutely not,' she said firmly. 'I said it loudly. Very loudly.'

'Right.' He nodded and rubbed a hand slowly along his

jaw. 'Because, you see, the thing is, I had the oddest dream about a woman who smelled of irises who did just that.'

'Intriguing dream.'

'It got better.'

For whom? 'Did it? How?'

'In my dream you—' he shot her a quick, lethal smile '—I'm sorry, I mean *she*—nearly kissed me.'

Abby stared at him, her heart practically leaping out of her chest because, oh, God, he *did* know. 'How strange,' she murmured, sounding mercifully calm even though her pulse was racing so fast it could have won the Grand National.

'Isn't it? So what with your scent and your actions, you can see why I think it might have been you.'

'Except that I'd never do anything so unprofessional.'

He arched an eyebrow. 'No?'

'Absolutely not.' It was his word against hers and she was sticking to hers like a limpet.

'Which presumably is why you didn't go through with it.'

'Utter nonsense.'

He shook his head slowly and tutted. 'There I was all vulnerable and defenceless—not to mention unconscious—and you were going to take advantage.'

Vulnerable and defenceless? Him? Hah. 'I was going to do no such thing.'

'And to think I was momentarily concerned that *my* integrity might have been compromised tonight,' he said, bulldozing her protests of innocence and hitting a nerve.

She narrowed her eyes. 'What are you implying?'

'We're even.'

He smiled and his eyes glinted and for the first time since she'd met him Abby got a glimpse of the man behind the façade, and immediately thought that she should have been careful what she wished for because she didn't know what to make of that glimpse. She thought she saw triumph and amusement, heat and desire, and despite her best efforts to prevent it her knees went weak with longing.

And then there was the intent. That just about robbed her of breath because his jaw was set, his eyes were fixed on her mouth and he was walking slowly towards her, and, idiot that she was, she was just standing there as if rooted to the spot.

'What are you doing?' she said shakily as he came to a stop half a foot from her.

'What we both want. What you chickened out of. No matter how much you protest to the contrary I know you're the woman of my dreams, Abby, and I'd like to realise those dreams.'

Oh, God, he was planning to kiss her and if he did she'd kiss him back. She knew she would. 'You said you weren't interested.'

'I lied. I'm interested.'

'No,' she breathed, managing to sound outraged, sexy and needy all at the same time, which so wasn't the plan.

'Why not?'

'I never mix business with pleasure,' she said, focusing on one of the founding principles of her company, albeit a bit belatedly.

'Neither do I. But the party's over and we no longer have business together.'

'We might. Hopefully.'

'If you were hired again you wouldn't be liaising directly with me. Or Jake. Tonight was a one-off.'

'I know that.'

'Well, then, what's the problem?'

'I have to work this afternoon.'

'What does that have to do with now?' he asked, his gaze roaming slowly, sensuously, over her features. 'All I'm suggesting is a kiss.'

Yeah, right. As if they'd stop at a kiss. As if she'd be able to. A kiss would be the beginning.

'You have a reputation,' she said, now beginning to sound as if she were clutching at straws, which she was because the longer she looked up into those mesmerising eyes, the more she was starting to forget her own name. He was overwhelming and she was floundering, drowning, way out of her league, her depth, her mind. And for someone who liked to be in control the knowledge that she wasn't was deeply unsettling.

'Doesn't everyone?'

'Yours is for being cold, ruthless and emotionally devoid.' The opposite of everything she believed in, in fact, and somehow, somewhere in the dim recesses of her mind, that seemed important.

'So?'

'Doesn't it bother you?'

'No. Does it bother you?'

'It doesn't do anything to me,' she said breathily. '*You* don't do anything to me.'

'Don't I?'

She shook her head and swallowed and wondered dizzily why she was still here when it would be so easy to leave. 'Not a thing.'

'See, now you've bruised my ego.'

'I dare say it'll bounce back.'

'I've no doubt it will. But in the meantime you make me want to prove you wrong.'

'What are you?' she said, her mouth bone dry and her heart pounding. 'Twelve?'

'Thirty-two.'

'Old enough not to have to prove anything to anyone, I'd have thought.'

He inched closer, so close she could feel the heat of his body, smell the scent of his skin, and her breath caught. 'True,' he murmured, and ran a finger down her cheek, making her shiver and burn at the same time. 'Nevertheless, before, when we were looking at each other and couldn't stop, I saw the desire in your eyes. I heard the subtle change in your breathing and I saw the blush in your cheeks. I want you and you want me and I don't see any point in denying it. Do you?'

Abby couldn't speak. All she could do was shake her head because, oh, what the hell, he was right, there wasn't any point at all. Not any more. Because he didn't do anything to her? Who was she kidding? She was a wreck, practically quivering with need, and it was blindingly obvious why she wasn't going anywhere.

'Therefore the only question that remains,' he continued in the same soft, seductive voice, 'is, what do you want to do about it?'

Even though her head was spinning with great big warning signs Abby knew exactly what she wanted to do about it. She wanted to tackle him to the floor, tear his clothes off, and hers, and then spend what was left of the night getting hot and sweaty with him.

And honestly, it was way too late to pull back now because she wasn't going anywhere and they both knew it. The time for fleeing had long gone. Kissing was inevitable. It had been since the moment they'd laid eyes on each other.

And as her resistance began to crumble beneath the force of the thrills that were racing through her Abby gave in. After all, it was only a kiss. What harm could come of a kiss? It wasn't as if she'd never kissed anyone before, was it? She had, loads of times, and the world hadn't stopped, so, honestly, what was she so worried about now? And what had she been doing thinking that one kiss would necessarily lead to something more? Of course it wouldn't. She was made of strong stuff. She could easily walk away afterwards if she wanted to. Easily.

'Oh, go on, then,' she said huskily with a mock dramatic sigh as desire began to thunder through her. 'If it really matters that much to you. I wouldn't want to be responsible for your dented ego.'

'Such enthusiasm,' he murmured with a smile.

'It's sufferance.'

He tutted and slowly shook his head. 'There you go again, Abby, making me want to prove you wrong.'

'So what are you waiting for?'

She lifted her chin and parted her lips and braced herself for the full force of him and the likely insides-melting impact it would have on her. But instead of going for her mouth, Leo put his hand on her jaw on one side of her face, and set his lips to the tiny spot beneath her ear on the other. It was the barest contact, a brush of air, a whisper, yet Abby gasped and trembled and, oh, dear, had that whimper been hers?

Apparently it had because she could feel his smile against her skin as he brushed his mouth against her jaw again, and she would have been prepared for the effect of it, only this time he didn't stop. Instead he trailed his mouth along her jaw while she just stood there, very probably swaying, her eyes fluttering closed as she gave in to the glorious sensations sweeping through her.

He slid his hand round to the back of her head, pulling her closer, and when his mouth did eventually find hers Abby moaned, wound her arms around his neck and gave up any hope of trying to rationalise this because all she could do was feel. Feel the heat of his mouth, the skilful strokes of his tongue, the hard muscles of his neck beneath her hands and the softness of his hair between her fingers.

As their kiss deepened, heated, she couldn't help arching her back to press herself closer, writhing against him a little and wishing she hadn't been so fastidious about doing up the buttons of her coat.

A sentiment that he seemed to share, because a second later he was easing away from her a fraction and with the hand that wasn't holding her head to his he deftly undid her buttons, parted her coat and then slid his arm round her back to pull her tight against him. And without the barrier of chunky wool she could feel the hard, thick length of his erection and nearly passed out with desire.

Leo moved his hand to her side, the edge of her breast, sending a shower of sparks cascading through her as he stroked her and suddenly kissing wasn't enough. She wanted to taste him all over. Get him naked. Push him down and feast. And touch. God, she wanted to touch.

Unwinding her hands from around his neck, she slipped them down his chest to the waistband of his trousers. She tugged his shirt up and out, slid her hands beneath, running her fingers over the hard muscles of his abdomen and then round, planting them on his lower back and exploring. His skin was smooth and hot and she couldn't get enough of it.

Until he wrenched his mouth from hers, breathing hard as he stared at her. 'Do you want to come upstairs with me?' he said hoarsely, his eyes blazing into hers with more heat and desire than she'd ever encountered.

Abby felt the room tilt as desire surged through her. 'To take a look at your etchings?'

'You've already seen my etchings.'

'You're right. I have.'

'So?'

Absolutely not, said her head. *You don't do this sort of thing.*

Definitely yes, said her body. *You need to do this sort of thing.*

And really there wasn't even that much of a battle because she was way beyond thinking straight. All she could think was that, unlike her crappy ex, here was a man who wasn't intimidated by her, here was a man who'd never accuse her of being too capable, and here was a man who could easily give her rock-bottom self-esteem the boost it needed.

The realisation blinded her, made her feel wanted, desirable, powerful for the first time in months, and it was a heady, intoxicating mix. And utterly, utterly irresistible.

'You know what?' she said as logic, reason and sense threw up their hands in defeat and ran for cover. 'I think I'd like to see some more.'

CHAPTER FIVE

However disorientated and dazed he'd been earlier, and however jet-lagged, Leo was clearly firing on all cylinders now because within a second of her agreement Abby found her bag being thrust at her, her hand being grabbed and herself being marched out of the room, then led down a labyrinth of deserted corridors that took them to his private lift.

He jabbed at the button, his jaw tight, not looking at her, as if not trusting himself not to take her then and there if he did. But once the doors had closed, cocooning them inside, totally cut off from the outside world, he pulled her to him, the look he gave her so full of heat and desire it nearly wiped out her knees, and kissed her. And by the time they were zooming up to his apartment she couldn't have said whether her ears were popping with the ascension or the dizzying effect of his mouth on hers.

Somewhere around perhaps the fourteenth floor he backed her up against the mirrored wall of the lift, pushed her dress up and then hitched her up. Supporting her weight with his upper body, he planted his hands at the backs of her thighs, lifted her legs and wrapped them round his waist.

Holding on tightly—although definitely not clinging—Abby caught sight of them in the mirrored wall opposite. Her coat flared around them, his big body hiding hers apart from her limbs entwined round him, and she didn't think she'd ever seen anything quite so erotic. Quite so wanton. And if the lift doors hadn't opened when they did she might not have been able to stop herself from begging him to take her right then and there.

As if she weighed nothing Leo carried her out and slammed her against the hall wall, making her drop her handbag and dislodging a picture, both of which landed with a soft thud on the floor.

Abby tore her mouth away from his, breathing hard as she looked at him. His eyes were so dark they were almost black, glazed with desire, and her stomach all but dissolved.

'What's the matter?' he said hoarsely.

'I think a Picasso just fell to the floor.'

'I'm sure he'd understand,' he said and resumed his assault on her jaw.

'Leo,' she said with a groan that was supposed to be of protest although it sounded more like one of desperation.

'Bedroom?'

'Yes. Quickly.'

Leo didn't waste a moment in complying and within seconds they were in his bedroom, tugging frantically at each other's clothing before coming to the evidently mutual conclusion that they could get naked more quickly if they concentrated on their own.

As Abby snapped off her belt and kicked off her shoes Leo's jacket hit the floor, followed swiftly by his shirt and bow tie. She slid down the zip of her dress and pushed it down so that it fell in a heap at her feet while Leo unbuttoned and unzipped his trousers and shoved them down and off, taking his socks and shoes with them.

She was so gripped with desire she barely gave the heap of crumpling clothes a moment's thought. The mess her hair must be in didn't cross her mind. Nor did the contents of her bag that were scattered all over the floor of the hall. Nothing mattered other than feeling his body against hers, his hands on her skin and his muscles beneath her palms just as soon as was humanly possible.

Once they'd stripped down to their underwear Leo reached for her and together they tumbled onto the bed, whereupon he rolled her beneath him and looked down at her, his eyes dark with molten heat and desire. 'I've been thinking about this all night,' he said roughly.

Her heart lurched at the thought that he'd been having as much trouble with her as she had been with him. 'So have I.'

'Earlier, when I woke up and saw you kneeling just over there I couldn't help imagining blindfolds—which aren't really my thing—and you, right here. On your knees. And as naked and as aroused as I was.'

Her breath caught and she swallowed. 'You were right,' she said softly. 'Before you woke up I did want to kiss you. More than that, I found myself imagining climbing onto the bed and having my wicked way with you.'

He frowned slightly. 'I don't understand it. We barely know each other.'

'I'm not sure chemistry cares much about that.'

'Perhaps not. This isn't just chemistry, though, is it? This is insanity.'

'I know. But right now, I have to confess I don't particularly care what it is.'

'Nor me.'

Then his head came down and she wound her arms around his neck and there were no more words, only hands and mouths and the sound of harsh, ragged panting.

She ran her hands all over his shoulders and down his back and felt him shudder beneath her touch. He reached round her back, deftly unclipped her strapless bra and then tugged it away from her and tossed it to the floor.

Without taking his mouth from hers, Leo moved his hand to her breast and she let out a low moan at the contact. Her skin was on fire, sparks were shooting through her and when his thumb stroked her nipple, she had to bite her lip to stop herself crying out.

She arched against him to increase the pressure and then he was pushing her back, replacing his hand with his mouth, and Abby moaned. She writhed, squirmed, but nothing she did could calm the fever raging through her, a fever that hit boiling point when he lifted his head, took her hands, stretched her arms above her head and wrapped her fingers around the bars of the bedhead.

'Let go and I'll stop,' he said, giving her a look that just about melted her insides before sliding down her body, his mouth trailing hot, burning kisses as he went. Lower and lower, over her ribcage, her abdomen, until he reached the top of her knickers where he stopped and she could feel his breath on her skin, coming hot and hard.

He put his hands on her hips, then slid them round and slipped his fingers through the band of lace. He pushed her knickers down and she lifted her hips to help. Once they were off, he twisted away to toss them in the same direction as her bra, and then turned his attention to peeling off her hold-ups, slowly rolling down first one, then the other, his hands sliding down her legs with deliberately slow, deliberately lingering thoroughness, leaving her weak with want.

And then he was back between her legs, his mouth hovering over the centre of her and she had to curl her fingers even more tightly around the bars because no way did she want him to stop, however tempting it was to let go, dig her hands into his hair and pull him tight against her.

And it was very tempting indeed, because he was dropping hot, searing kisses on her inner thighs, her hip bones, everywhere but where she wanted him, teasing her, tormenting her, driving her nuts. She closed her eyes and bit her lip with frustration but she was damned if she was going to beg. She had self-control. Gallons of the stuff. It was in her bones, her very marrow. She could handle anything.

But then, just when she felt like screaming with frustration, he touched his mouth to her and Abby wondered who she'd been kidding because her self-control unravelled and sensation, hot and sizzling and mind-blowing, rocked through her.

With his lips, his tongue and his clever, *clever* fingers he licked and sucked and delved and she gave up trying to think. What was the point when she didn't have to think about a thing? Leo seemed to know exactly what he was doing and that was too rare to not appreciate as fully as possible.

So she was going to appreciate. And feel. Ooh, how she could feel...

Every inch of her body was on fire. Alive and tingling and tightening. The heat of him, the touch of him and his skill at this sent arrows of heat and pleasure darting through her, sharper and harder and faster until she couldn't hold back, couldn't cling on any longer and, crying out his name as she came, she broke apart, the pleasure rushing through her, swamping her, making her forget everything but him.

It took minutes for her heart rate to subside. A few more before her breathing was back to normal. Yet the lovely feeling of satiation lingered right up until she felt Leo prop himself up on an elbow and began trailing a hand from her collarbone to her stomach and back again, over and over. And then desire was blooming again, heat was flooding her body and her heart rate was once more on the up.

'Please tell me you have condoms,' she murmured, not quite able to look him in the eye after what he'd just done to her.

'I do.' Abandoning her torso, he twisted around to open a drawer in the bedside table, grabbed a handful and dropped them beside the lamp. 'Enough?' he asked, his face dark and his jaw tight.

'I should think so,' she said, shivers running through her all over again at the intensity she could feel radiating off him. 'Can I help myself?'

'Be my guest.'

Pushing him gently so he lay on his back, Abby reached across him to take one, and looked at it with raised eyebrows.

'Strawberry?' she murmured, a bit surprised because Leo didn't seem like the flavoured condom kind of man. He seemed like the kind of man who wouldn't care about anything other than the fact the condom did the job it was designed to do.

'Stag night.'

'Sounds eventful.'

'It wasn't.'

'Lucky me.'

'In what way?'

'I love strawberries,' she said, shooting him a wicked smile.

His breath caught and then he let it out, long and slow. 'That is lucky.'

Straddling him, Abby leaned forwards, angled her head and kissed him, tasting herself on his tongue and shivering. He clamped a hand to the back of her neck and, with the other, pressed her hips down so that she fitted around the hot, hard length of him, still confined by his shorts. He tilted his pelvis, pressing against her, and she groaned. She gently circled her hips and then it was his turn to groan.

Feeling almost dizzy with the need to have him inside her, Abby eased out of his grip and with his help divested him of his shorts. Unable to resist the desire to find out what he felt like, she curled her fingers around him, and moved her hand slowly up and then even more slowly down, feeling him harden further, strain against her fingers, hearing him swear.

'Abby,' he said warningly.

'What?' she said.

'Don't.'

With some reluctance, she let him go, settled herself between his legs and carefully tore open the foil packet. She extracted the condom and, pressing the tip of her tongue to the end of it, put the whole thing in her mouth.

As she closed her mouth she heard him inhale sharply, and she glanced up at him to see him watching her intently, his jaw rigid. Then she leaned down, held him steady and opened her mouth over him, using her tongue and her lips to roll the condom on in one smooth practised move.

'Jesus,' he breathed, his voice gratifyingly hoarse. 'Neat trick.'

She straightened and grinned at the way his eyes had glazed over. 'A staple in the repertoire of any self-respecting tart, I'd have thought.'

'You should consider a career change. You'd make a fortune.'

'I already do. My turnover last year was over three million pounds.'

'Profit?'

'Gross or net?'

'Doesn't matter. Either.'

'Two point five. Gross.'

'Tidy.'

She tilted her head and smiled. 'Numbers turn you on, don't they?'

His eyes glittered. 'That thing you just did turns me on. You turn me on. Especially on the dance floor. The numbers are just the icing on the cake.'

He reached for her and kissed her and, dizzy with longing, Abby moaned into his mouth. He held her tighter, kissed her harder, and, unable to wait any longer, she reached between them, took him in her hand and sank slowly down onto him, groaning as her body took him in, adjusting to his size and then revelling in it.

'My net profit,' she murmured into his ear when he was lodged deep inside her, 'was just under two.'

'Enough,' he growled, clamping her hips to him, then

lifting his knee and rolling her over so that she lay beneath him, pinned to the bed by his big powerful body and his dark, intense gaze.

He lowered his head and kissed her and then began to move, slowly pulling out of her and then thrusting back, rolling his hips as she lifted her legs and wound them around his waist, and there was now nothing but searing heat and clamouring desire and the powerful, intoxicating journey to release.

Supporting himself on his elbows, Leo held her head in his hands as they kissed and moved together, and despite the thick fog in her head, the desire swirling through her that was growing stronger and stronger, she felt oddly cherished.

But she didn't have time to wonder about it, wonder whether she should be concerned about it, because Leo was upping the pace and she couldn't think about anything but the way he was making her feel. Electric and on fire and so very nearly there.

He was driving faster, harder, deeper. She could see the pulse hammering at the base of his neck, could feel the tension bunching the muscles of his shoulders, and could feel her response to it. Her body was tightening, the pleasure spiralling, the release she so desperately craved tantalisingly close yet still agonisingly out of reach.

And then he reached down, wound an arm around her lower back and tilted her pelvis, drove into her hard and deep and without warning she came, hard and fierce and long, her insides unravelling and stars exploding behind her eyelids as she gasped for breath and shook with pleasure, just as with a harsh groan Leo erupted inside her, pulsing into her and setting off a flurry of aftershocks that had her trembling and convulsing around him all over again.

How long they lay there Abby had no idea. She was too busy recovering from the most intense orgasm of her life to even think about looking at her watch. Too busy wondering whether her heart might have suffered permanent damage from all the extra beating it had done. Too busy thinking, cherished? Cherished? What utter, sentimental heat-of-the-moment rubbish.

But eventually Leo lifted himself up, and stared down at her, looking as blown away as she felt, his eyes and his expression, for once, not shuttered. 'Well, that proves a point, don't you think?' he muttered hoarsely, brushing a damp lock of hair off her forehead and frowning slightly as he tucked it behind her ear.

'Possibly,' she said, her breathing going skittery and her mouth drying at the caress. 'But what exactly, and to whom?'

'God knows.'

He shook his head as if to clear it, and she could feel the movement along the length of his body. On top of her. Inside her. It made her shiver, made her want more.

'Maybe in a quest for clarity,' she said, her heart beginning to pound against her ribs as heat wound through her, 'we should try it again.'

'Excellent thinking,' he muttered and bent his head to kiss her.

Clarity might not have been achieved—despite the number of condoms they'd got through—but one very good point, thought Leo, yawning, rubbing a hand over his face and reading Abby's note, was that whatever last night had been about, apart from endless and scorchingly hot, they weren't done. Not nearly.

Apparently she'd left at ten this morning. She'd therefore been out of his bed for—he picked up his watch and glanced at it—approximately seven hours, but he wanted her back in it. Now.

Sitting up and dropping the note on the bedside table where he'd found it, Leo stretched to ease the not unwelcome ache in his muscles and wished she were there to relieve the ache in an altogether different part of his anatomy.

She should have woken him. He wouldn't have minded. He had no plans for the weekend other than getting over jet lag, and so closing the curtains, shutting the door, blocking out everything but Abby for the next day or two would have reset his body clock nicely.

He wouldn't have minded if she'd left a phone number either, but she hadn't, although that obstacle wasn't altogether insurmountable. If he wanted to call her, he could.

The question was, did he?

Despite what his brother might think he hadn't exactly been a monk since his near miss of a marriage—he'd just been discreet and careful—but generally his relationships with women over the last five or so years had been short. As in less than twenty-four hours short, which suited him perfectly because he wasn't interested in engagement of anything other than the physical kind.

The very thought of it, of having to actually talk to the women he took to bed, or, worse, have them trying to get to know him, brought him out in hives, so discreet, mutually beneficial one-night stands had always been fine with him. They scratched an itch, offered a distraction, relaxation, and, more importantly, never left him wanting more.

Abby, however, for some reason, did. Not a lot more, obviously, because a relationship was absolutely out of the question. He'd tried it once and look what had happened. His feelings had been trampled, his heart had been sliced into ribbons and his pride decimated.

However, another night he could probably handle. Maybe even two. And he probably needed them, actually, because the strength of his desire for her was undeniable. It was also odd. Unusual. A bit unnerving but strangely exhilarating.

As was Abby, because he didn't think he'd ever come across anyone quite so open, so uninhibited, in the bedroom.

To his surprise but delight, she'd had no qualms about telling him what worked for her and what didn't, and she'd gone along with his suggestions with enthusiasm. Not sufferance. Enthusiasm. And a hell of a lot of it.

All of which was, apparently, addictive, because even though it went against his modus operandi of late he was up for more of it. Literally. And bordering on painfully.

The night had been fun, unexpectedly so, and he wanted a repeat, so would seeing her again *really* be that much of an issue?

Of course it wouldn't, he told himself, contemplating with a faint grimace the ice-cold shower he was going to have to take in Abby's absence. He might want her more than any other woman he'd taken to bed recently, but even so, because he was no longer susceptible to any member of the opposite sex, she posed absolutely no threat to his peace of mind. No woman would ever again, so the niggling suspicion that *she* somehow *could* was simply jet lag messing with his head.

And anyway, just because he'd like to see her again it didn't mean he was embarking on anything, did it? It wasn't as if he'd have to actually talk to her much, was it? No. Judging by the way things had gone last night, Abby seemed to be the 'less talking more action' type, which was, happily, exactly *his* type.

So he'd call her up and suggest they get together. Tonight, if she was free after whatever work she had to do. Or tomorrow. Whenever. But soon.

Spying his clothes, which from memory he'd left in a heap on the floor beside the bed but were now draped neatly over the back of the armchair that sat in the corner of the room, Leo got up and headed over in search of his phone. His shoes were positioned together at the foot of the chair, and as he rummaged around his trouser pocket for his phone he smiled slightly and wondered whether he'd find his socks and shorts in the laundry basket in the bathroom.

Thinking that after her abandon on the dance floor and last night's subsequent private performance he'd *never* have had her down as a neat freak, he pulled out his phone and saw that he had had three missed calls and two new voice-mail messages from his brother and a text from his mother.

Well, they could wait, he thought, bringing up a search engine with a couple of quick taps. He had a phone number to find and an entirely different call to make.

CHAPTER SIX

'OH, MY GOD, you *slept* with a *client*?'

At the astonishment in her best friend's voice Abby consulted her clipboard needlessly and wondered if she'd done the right thing in telling Gemma everything that had gone on last night.

It had seemed like an excellent idea when they'd sat down with a cup of tea in the huge kitchen/diner of the posh Kensington house five minutes ago—firstly because she and Gemma had met years back at the catering company they'd both once worked for, were closer than sisters and knew practically everything there was to know about each other, and secondly because after spending the entire day thinking about it she'd had to tell someone before she burst—but now she sort of regretted it.

While the memory remained hers alone she could label it a fantasy, revisit it whenever she fancied and in the meantime continue to deny to herself that she'd ever behaved so wantonly. Had ever lost control quite so spectacularly and, even worse, enjoyed it all quite so much.

Putting it out there made her behaviour and her loss of control irrefutable. It made the whole encounter real, available for dissection and analysis and she wasn't sure she wanted either. Which was unfortunate because Gemma relished both.

'Strictly speaking there wasn't a lot of sleeping involved,' said Abby, abandoning her clipboard because she knew perfectly well from the checks she'd carried out ten minutes ago that the catwalk was complete and secure and the make-up artist, the costumier, the DJ and the photographer were all good to go. 'And technically he wasn't a client at that point, but essentially, yes.'

'After meeting him what, six hours earlier?'

She took a quick sip of strong but not nearly fortifying enough tea. 'Thereabouts.'

Gemma shook her head in disbelief, her eyes wide with shock. 'Wow. I think I need something considerably stronger than tea.'

'Tell me about it.' No amount of coffee and tea could make up for the fact that she'd had little more than two hours' sleep last night. Tequila, on the other hand, would work nicely. Shame it was only half past five in the afternoon and she was working.

'That's something *I* normally do,' said Gemma. 'Not you.'

'I know.'

'And even I draw the line at clients.'

'I know.'

'So come on, then, what happened?'

'I don't really know,' said Abby, still a bit bemused by it all even though she'd thought about little else in the intervening hours. 'One minute we were talking, then we were kissing and five minutes later we were in bed.'

Although it hadn't been quite that simple, had it? The talking had been laden with subtext, the kissing had been mind-blowing and as for the bed bit, well, that had been explosive. So actually, factoring in the misunderstandings earlier in the evening and the subsequent questioning of her integrity, it had all been rather complicated.

'And how was it?'

'Fine.'

'Fine?' Gemma said, a smile slowly spreading across her face. 'That's all? If it was just "fine", then why did you stick around to do it six times?'

'OK, then, it was great.' Which was still a total understatement for how it had been, because she couldn't re-member a night like it. When she'd finally managed to drag herself out of his bed this morning she'd barely been able to walk. A hot shower in Leo's en suite had helped but, even now, pretty much every time she moved she could feel mus-cles she didn't even know she had pinging and lingering traces of heat and pleasure shimmering through her.

'Then it was probably just what you needed,' said Gemma, dragging her back to the present. 'Especially after Martin.'

Abby shuddered at the thought of her ex, who'd accused her of being undateable by way of being intimidating, overly self-reliant and, of all things, too capable. 'Definitely.'

'He was a jerk.'

'He was.'

'I mean, how can anyone be "too capable"?' grumbled Gemma, voicing a grievance that was familiar to both of them.

'And what am I supposed to do about it anyway?' said Abby. 'Dumb down? Pretend I can't put up a shelf or change a tyre or something and feign ignorance when someone men-tions quantitative easing, just in case I hurt some poor man's feelings?'

Gemma shuddered. 'I wouldn't.'

'Neither would I.'

'I bet you wouldn't have to with Leo.' Gemma sighed and fanned her face. 'I'm deadly envious, you know. I mean, he's successful, rich and hot.' She stopped, considered, then added, 'Although not as hot as Jake, clearly, but still.'

Abby stared at her friend. 'Jake? Seriously?'

'Yes, seriously. Leo might have the whole brooding, enig-matic thing going on, but give me that melt-your-knickers charm any day. He's delicious.'

'Leo's not just brooding and enigmatic. He's imaginative, too,' Abby couldn't help saying as the finer details of some of what they'd got up to flashed into her head.

'And now I'm even more envious.'

Abby grinned and put down her teacup. 'Sorry.'

'You know, now I think about it,' Gemma mused, 'I wondered if there was something going on between you two.'

'What on earth do you mean? We didn't speak. We didn't meet. We didn't even look at each other.'

'Exactly,' said Gemma with a triumphant grin. 'You spoke to Jake plenty, yet you studiously avoided Leo. And you know, I happened to see you on the dance floor on my way back from taking a whole load of plates to the van. Did you notice the way he was looking at you when you were dancing?'

'Not really,' she said, choosing to gloss over the charged moment their gazes had clashed. 'How was he looking at me?'

'I have no idea. His face was totally blank, yet he couldn't take his eyes off you. Who knows what was going through his head? I had no clue and I consider myself something of an expert when it comes to men. It was weird.'

'Talking of which, have you heard from—?' Abby broke off and racked her brains for the name of the man who was the flavour of the week but drew a blank.

'Bob?'

'Bob.'

Gemma sighed and shook her head. 'Nope. So there's a surprise.'

'I'm sorry.'

She shrugged. 'That's how it goes, right?'

'It doesn't have to.'

'So you keep saying, but one of these days I'll meet someone who'll actually call after we've done the deed. I know I will.'

Abby, who was familiar with the pattern of old and had had to pick up the pieces more times than she could remember, doubted it but she bit her lip because this wasn't either the time or place to try and persuade her friend to perhaps re-evaluate some of her lifestyle choices.

'Maybe whoever comes along next will be the one,' she said, hoping against hope that he would be but knowing it was unlikely.

'Maybe he will. But, anyway, enough about my rubbish track record. You and Leo Cartwright are far more interesting.'

'Are we?'

'Don't be coy. When are you going to see him again?'

'I'm not.'

Gemma's jaw dropped and her cup clattered in the saucer. 'What? Are you insane? Why on earth not?'

Abby set her jaw and reminded herself that she was doing the right thing even though her body, which clearly agreed with Gemma, was doing its damnedest to get her to change her mind. 'Well, for one thing, I didn't leave my phone number.'

'Idiot,' said Gemma, who gave her number to pretty much every man she met, with limited success. 'I wouldn't have thought you'd make such a schoolgirl error.'

Abby shook her head. 'No error,' she said. 'I did it deliberately.'

'Whatever for?'

'It seemed a bit desperate,' she said pointedly.

'All's fair in love and war,' said Gemma sagely, 'and, believe me, if you don't try and snap him up someone else will.'

'Then they're welcome to him.'

Gemma frowned. 'Do you regret it?'

'Not for a moment. Why would I? I feel fabulous. Martin? Martin who?'

'Then you're nuts, you know that?'

'Look,' said Abby, getting up to refill her cup from the urn, 'if Leo wants to get in touch he can get hold of my number and call me easily enough—it is on my website after all—but there really wouldn't be any point even if he did.'

'If the night was as great as you say it was it seems to me that there's a mutually very good point indeed.'

'It wouldn't go anywhere.'

'How do you know that, you pessimist?'

Abby sighed and thought about the information she'd dug up on him after half an hour on Google, some of which had been so well buried—although how he'd managed that she had no idea—she'd very nearly missed it. 'Because he's about as emotionally repressed as they come.'

'Ah,' said Gemma with a slow nod of dawning realisation. 'Right. I see.'

'So it doesn't matter how great he is in bed,' said Abby. 'He's not my type at all.'

'Well, OK, but don't you think you may be jumping to conclusions? I mean, you don't exactly know him very well, do you? At least not in anything other than the physical sense.'

'I get the feeling you could have known him for years and still not really know him.'

'That's true of most men, I should think.'

'Possibly, but, as you so astutely pointed out, I was keeping my eye on him last night and the entire time he was there but not there if you know what I mean.'

'Keeping his distance.'

'Exactly.'

'It was work.'

'True, but Jake said it was impossible to know what he was thinking, and what about the weird way he was watching me?'

'Yes, that was odd.'

'And then there's his reputation. That doesn't come from nowhere. There has to be a basis for it.'

'Maybe.'

Abby leaned towards Gemma and lowered her voice a little, even though what with the family getting ready upstairs there was no one within earshot. 'I also subsequently found out something that would suggest that he takes bottling things up to the extreme.'

'Like what?'

'Like he was nearly married once.'

Gemma's eyes widened. 'Really?'

Abby nodded.

'Blimey. I hadn't heard that.'

'That's my point.'

'What happened?'

'Well, from what I can gather it was around Christmas five years ago. He was jilted. At the last minute. Literally at the altar.'

'Heavens.'

'I know. Apparently his fiancée decided she was too in love with an old flame she'd hooked up with again on Facebook to go through with it.'

Gemma winced. 'Ouch. That has to have hurt.'

Abby nodded. 'You'd think so, wouldn't you? Yet when he said that he didn't particularly like this time of year all he mentioned was the commercialism of it and the lack of business opportunity.'

'Well, to be fair to him, what else would you have expected? He'd hardly have spilled all the details to a complete stranger. Who would?'

'No, but you'd have thought there'd at least be a flicker of, I don't know, *something*.' Abby shook her head at the memory of how cool he'd been about it. How smoothly the excuses had slid off his tongue. How quickly. How practised the lack of emotion had seemed. 'But he came across as being so totally unfazed by it.'

'Maybe he is.'

'But then why would he still be hung up over the time-of-year thing?'

Gemma frowned. 'Hmm. You have a point. But how come we didn't know about this? In fact, how come no one knows about this? I'd have thought it would have provided enough fodder for the gossip mags to keep going for months.'

'Well, quite. But all I found was an engagement announcement and then a tiny five-line article about what had happened and how the wedding had been called off. On an obscure blog somewhere. It didn't appear anywhere in the press, so the whole thing must have somehow been hushed up or something.'

'Crikey.'

As her belt began to ring and vibrate Abby extracted her phone, glanced down at the unknown number and hit the silence button before sticking it back in the pouch.

'Anyway,' she said, making a note on her clipboard to check and call back once she'd got through this London's Next Top Tween Model birthday party, 'the point is that while I wouldn't mind a boyfriend, the last thing I need is to get involved with someone who bottles everything up. All that second-guessing and getting it wrong...' She grimaced as thoughts of her family and their total inability to communicate spun through her head. 'So not my bag.'

'I suppose not. But I still think you're making a mistake.'

'Better now than later,' said Abby lightly, determinedly putting Leo and last night from her mind because she really didn't need the distraction right now, or ever. 'Besides, if anything more *did* happen between us I'd only end up wanting to be the one to change him and we know how well *that* works out.'

'We do.'

'Not well at all because men don't want to be changed. And I can understand that. I don't really want to be changed either.'

'Who does?'

Silence fell for a moment as the relationships of Abby's youth flickered through her head and maybe Gemma's flickered through hers, and then she froze. 'Oh, no.'

'What?'

'I have a horrible feeling I've forgotten to put those Chanel nail varnishes in the going home bags.'

'You? Forget something? Impossible.'

'Improbable but not impossible after only a couple of hours of sleep. I'd better go and check.'

Her friend shook her head and tutted. 'Designer lipsticks, nail varnishes and face creams… Whatever happened to a piece of cake and a balloon?'

'Happily for us they went the same way as jelly, crisps and pin the tail on the donkey,' said Abby with a quick grin as she stood up and put her teacup on the pristine granite work surface. 'If you need a hand counting the carrot sticks or spooning out the hummus, just shout.'

For someone who'd almost managed to convince himself that he wasn't in the slightest bit bothered by the fact that Abby had neither answered his call nor got back to him, Leo wasn't doing a very good job of following through.

He'd left a message asking her to call him when she had a moment, and had then sat down at his desk with every intention of putting in a couple of hours of work on the financial details of a development project the company was undertaking in China.

Half an hour later, however, during which he'd achieved nothing but a full-blown rerun of the night before and consequently a hard-on that would not subside, he'd given up, stalked into the gym and run twenty miles on the treadmill. But that hadn't done anything to restore the order he was so badly missing either.

Nor had the rugby match he'd watched on television or the drinks he'd just had with a couple of friends.

While his phone was rarely out of reach, Leo didn't generally have too much trouble ignoring it. Yet this evening he hadn't been able to stop looking at it, whether while sitting pointlessly at his desk, pounding out the miles or knocking back the beer.

A dozen times he'd checked the volume setting, the battery, the signal, all of which were, of course, perfectly fine, and earlier he'd even tried calling himself from the landline, just in case there was a connection problem. There wasn't, naturally, as proven by the calls and texts he'd received from practically everyone he knew but her, and his inability to move on and concentrate on something—anything—else was driving him insane.

It was absurd, he told himself, gritting his teeth as he once again found himself at his desk, staring blankly at his computer screen while thoughts of Abby filled his head. Anyone would think he was desperate to hear from her. And he wasn't. Much. It was just that he didn't like things hanging, un-dealt-with. Didn't like the feeling of not being in control and at the mercy of someone else's whim.

But what choice did he have, short of calling her again, which he was absolutely not going to do? Besides, she'd told him she had to work, which was obviously what she was doing. He presumed the number he'd called her on was her work one, so, professional as she was, she'd get back to him when she could. He'd just have to be patient.

The call she had rejected earlier had been from Leo.

Back at home after a successful but exhausting evening, Abby tapped her phone against her mouth and wondered why a brief message asking her to ring him back would warrant such a quickening of her heart rate and the heat that was surging through her.

Hadn't she decided that he wasn't her type? Hadn't she convinced herself that she wanted to have nothing more to do with him? She had, so why was she getting so hot and bothered about a ten-second voicemail message? Why did his deep voice in her ear seem so very intimate? Why was it so difficult to wipe last night from her memory? And what did he want?

There was only one way to find out, so, with her heart beating annoyingly fast, Abby silenced the episode of *St Jude's* she'd pre-recorded and had been watching before she'd suddenly remembered the missed call and took a fortifying gulp of wine.

Was ten too late to ring? Should she send a message instead? No, better to get this over and done with. If it was too late, all that would happen was that he wouldn't answer. She could leave a message and the ball would be back in his court.

Putting her glass down, Abby crossed her legs, sat back and hit the button to return his call. He answered practically before the phone had time to ring, robbing her of the second or two of mental reinforcement she could have done with.

'Abby,' he said, his deep voice making her stomach do that weird swooping thing once again.

She took a deep breath and swallowed hard in an effort to avoid the breathiness that seemed to invade her voice whenever she spoke to him. 'Hi.'

'How are you?'

'Fine. You?'

'Good.'

'I hope it's not too late to be calling.'

'Not at all.'

'I'm sorry for not getting back to you sooner. I was working.'

'How did it go?'

'Fine.' *Way to go with the verbal skills, Abby,* she thought, mentally rolling her eyes and pulling herself together because she really ought to be able to handle small talk with someone whose body she'd explored at length. 'I mean, as fine as twenty ten-year-old wannabe supermodels can be.'

'Ten-year-old supermodels?'

She heard the surprise in his voice and could imagine him sitting there, eyebrows up as the ghost of a smile played at his mouth. His mouth... Sexy, clever, and so very damn good at kissing...

'Abby?' he said and she snapped out of her delicious little reverie.

'What can I say?' she said, and, oh, heavens, the breathiness was back. 'The client asks and I provide.'

There was a heavy pause during which she, and presumably he, remembered exactly how he'd asked and how she'd provided, and Abby gave herself a good pinch. And gasped at the pain because she hadn't meant to pinch herself quite so hard.

'Are you all right? What happened?'

'Nothing. I'm right as rain,' she said. 'Sorry. Banged into the coffee table. How's the jet lag?'

'Going.'

'That must be a relief.'

'You have no idea. Thank you for your note.'

'You're welcome.' *You're welcome?* God.

'I take it you got home all right this morning.'

She couldn't say 'fine' again, and in any case it hadn't been fine. 'After a fashion.'

'What do you mean?'

'My car had been towed. I had to take a taxi to the pound and get it released.' After two hours' sleep with her hair a mess and her party clothes rumpled. Not exactly a good look.

'Oh, dear.'

'Hmm. It was a walk of shame I definitely wouldn't care to repeat.'

There was another silence. 'Walk of shame?'

'Just an expression,' she clarified quickly because she could hear the frown in his tone and she didn't want him thinking she regretted what they'd done because she didn't. 'I have no shame.'

'Neither do I,' he said, then after a pause, added, 'Which leads me to the reason I'm calling.'

For some reason her pulse sped up. 'Oh?'

'I'd like to see you again.'

For a moment sheer delight soared through her, and then it plummeted because it couldn't happen, and oh, dear, was this going to be awkward?

'Look, Leo,' she said, concentrating on his emotional repression and strengthening her resolve because despite knowing he was wrong for her she badly wanted to say yes. 'Last night was great and everything, but I don't think it should happen again.'

There was a pause. A bit too long, a bit too uncomfortable, and she wondered if he was still there.

'Really?' he said eventually, and it struck her that some of the warmth had gone from his voice. 'Out of interest, why?'

Hmm. She could hardly tell him she suspected he had a problem with expressing his feelings while she was all for it, and that that difference of approach made anything between them a no-no. He'd think she was mad. 'Because it should never really have happened in the first place,' she said. 'I admit it's a pretty grey area, but I still have an issue with mixing business and pleasure and on reflection I think we fall into that category.'

'You didn't seem to mind last night.'

'No, well, you caught me by surprise.'

'Likewise. But you needn't worry,' he drawled, 'because I didn't actually mean it like that.'

'Oh,' said Abby, feeling herself sort of deflate, which didn't make any sense because she ought to be glad he didn't mean it 'like that'. She wasn't interested in him, was she? Which was just as well, because apparently, in spite of a night of hot sex—or maybe because of it—she still wasn't dateable. 'Then what did you mean?' she said, reminding herself that Martin had been a prat and she absolutely didn't care what he thought of her.

'I'd like to see you to discuss some business.'

Business. Of course. 'I see,' she said, her voice mercifully reflecting none of the emotion that was churning through her. 'When?'

'Tomorrow?'

'Tomorrow's Sunday.'

'Is that a problem?'

Apart from it being the first full day off she'd had in weeks? 'No, no problem.'

'Good,' he said crisply, all business. 'My office? Say four?'

'See you then.'

CHAPTER SEVEN

AT THREE-THIRTY the following afternoon, Leo was pacing around his office in something of a panic. Which was an unusual state of affairs for him because he was generally way too cool-headed and in command of himself to panic, but then nothing about any of his dealings with Abby so far had been usual.

Up until he'd met her, for example, he'd never wanted to extend a one-night stand. He'd never hung around waiting for the phone to ring like some poor pathetic idiot and then jumped on it the minute she had. He'd never gone into his office on a Sunday.

He'd certainly never invented 'business' that needed urgent discussion when there wasn't any.

But what else was he to have done when she'd told him going out with him was not going to happen? Tell her he couldn't stop thinking about her? About what they'd done? Humiliate himself even further than he already had by begging her for more? Hah. Not a bloody chance.

Grinding his teeth, Leo resumed his pacing and scowled down at the carpet. It had never occurred to him that she wouldn't want a repeat of Friday night. If he was brutally honest he hadn't given what she might want much thought at all. But if he had he'd have been confident she'd say yes, because why would she say no when they'd had such a good time?

Yet 'no' was exactly what she'd said.

So what had put her off him? Had he said something, done something? Since their call last night he'd racked his brains to work it out but had drawn a blank. He presumed she had her reasons and he ought to be fine with that because it wasn't as if he'd never had great sex before and it wasn't as if he wouldn't have it again.

Annoyingly, though, he wasn't fine with it. He hated rejection. And he wasn't used to it. Ever since Lisa had jilted him at the altar and made him a laughing stock he'd taken great care to avoid it, never ever putting himself in a position where it could happen, which was why the women he slept with generally approached him first.

So that was another exception to the general pre-Abby state of affairs because she was the first woman in a very long time he'd firstly actively made the first move on and secondly had planned on asking out. And, boy, what a mistake that had been because nearly twenty-four hours on and her rejection was still stinging.

So what he'd been thinking creating a different excuse to see her when she didn't want to have anything more to do with him he had no idea. He'd wanted to save face, but with hindsight he must have been out of his mind because he'd been racking his brains all day yet hadn't been able to come up with a single bit of business he could possibly have to discuss with her.

Professionally there was nothing on the horizon that sprang to mind. No openings, no celebrations, nothing. And, anyway, if he *did* manage to drum something work-related up, it would no doubt be so spurious that his brother would be on it like a terrier, wondering at his sudden interest in the role that Jake usually played and undoubtedly coming to all kinds of—probably accurate—conclusions. All of which was about as appealing as a kick in the balls.

He couldn't think of anything personal either. He generally loathed parties and now rarely threw any himself. After the hideously mortifying debacle that had been his wedding day, the mere thought of being centre of attention again brought him out in a cold sweat.

None of his friends was getting married so there were no stag nights to sort out. Jake's birthday wasn't until November, and, as he'd just turned thirty, the next one wasn't significant enough to warrant a full-blown party the likes of which would need an organiser like Abby. His own birthday was months away, and, again, wasn't a major one.

The obvious solution would have been to call Abby back and cancel, but for some reason something had stopped him from doing that. Every time he picked up the phone he just couldn't bring himself to do it. Somehow it seemed to smack of cowardice, weakness, indecision, and having told her he had business to discuss with her, what possible reason could he give for now not?

As a result, for the first time in years Leo was in one hell of a mess. Abby was about to pitch up any moment expecting to be asked to organise something, and he didn't have a clue what.

Hell.

He shoved his hands through his hair and ran through the options all over again. Work? No. Friends? No. Jake? No. So what was left? His parents? Nope. They were in their early sixties and there was nothing significant going on there. Aunts? Uncles? Cousins? Neighbours? Pets?

Pets? Damn. That was really scraping the barrel, especially since the only pets he knew of were the flock of hens his father had given his mother on their last wedding anniversary.

Although, hang on…

Wait one tiny little moment…

Leo froze, mid pace, backtracking frantically and zooming in on the thought dancing around in the shadows of his mind.

Hadn't the hens arrived in spring? Therefore, wasn't his

parents' anniversary coming up sometime soon? March? April, maybe? And hadn't there been thirty-nine of the flapping, clucking things?

With his heart going like a steam train and his brain spinning like a top, he did the calculations and punched the air in relief and triumph because...yes, this spring, his parents had been married forty unimaginably long but presumably happy years.

Heaven only knew how they'd done it—he'd fallen before the first hurdle, namely the church, and had no intention of ever going remotely near an altar again—but nevertheless, halle-bloody-lujah, because if forty years of marriage weren't worth celebrating, weren't worth the kind of party that needed an organiser, then he didn't know what was.

Deciding that Leo wasn't the man for her was all very well in theory and all very logical and rational and satisfyingly sensible but unfortunately Abby's body wasn't having any of it.

No. Her body, treacherous being that it was, remembered with unforgiving clarity exactly what she and Leo had done together and how fantastic he'd made her feel, and was demanding more.

It didn't matter that they hadn't touched, that he'd barely looked at her since she'd walked through the door. Just one look at him and she'd wanted to march right up to him and kiss him senseless.

So much for the pep talk she'd given herself on the drive over, during which she'd told herself to focus on business at all times. And so much for the assumption that the chemistry that had surged between them on Friday night had been nothing more than a blip, brought on by fatigue, adrenalin and the thrill of success. She'd underestimated the force of his presence and the efficiency of her memory. Big time.

But it would be fine, she'd told herself, removing her coat and hanging it up, then taking the seat he'd indicated. It had to be. In well-worn jeans, white shirt and chocolate-brown jacket and leaning back against the edge of his desk, he might be looking unbelievably sexy but that wasn't important.

This afternoon wasn't about contemplating a repeat of Friday night, however tempting it was to leap up, push him back over his desk and climb on top of him. This was all about business, and it was high time she channelled the professional he was expecting instead of the seductress he surely wasn't.

Ruthlessly stamping out the desire simmering away deep inside her and reminding herself that whatever had gone on between them before, it was over and Leo was now nothing more than a potential client, she gave herself a quick shake, plastered a bright smile to her face and was just trying to think of something to break the oddly unnerving silence when he spoke.

'Thank you for giving up your Sunday afternoon to meet me,' he said. 'I appreciate it.'

'No problem,' said Abby with a polite smile since politeness was obviously the way this afternoon was going to go. 'On the phone you said you had business to discuss so what can I do for you, Mr Cartwright?'

She thought she caught a flicker of something in his eyes and a slight tightening of his jaw but both were so fleeting that she figured she must have been imagining things.

'*Mr* Cartwright?' he echoed, his eyebrows lifting although his expression and eyes remained inscrutable in a way that she was beginning to recognise.

'This is business.'

'Nevertheless, it's a bit late for such formality, don't you think?' he said, his gaze skating over her for a second and igniting the heat she'd been doing so well to bank. 'Especially given how well we know each other.'

Abby set her jaw and concentrated on not thinking about how well they knew each other, carnally at least, because she really *wasn't* going there again, not physically, not even mentally. 'Whatever you say. Leo.'

He tilted his head and smiled faintly at her. 'Abby,' he said, and despite her best intentions she immediately thought of the way he'd growled her name in her ear while buried deep inside her.

'So?' she said, lifting her chin and determinedly blocking it out.

'I'd like you to sort something out for my parents' fortieth wedding anniversary.'

Oh. For some reason, Abby was taken aback. She hadn't been expecting something social. She'd been thinking corporate. She really didn't know why. Maybe it was that he seemed so remote and so icy cool she couldn't imagine him having friends and enjoying himself. She certainly couldn't imagine him having parents.

'Well?' he prompted. 'Would that be something you could do?'

Abby snapped back and pulled herself together. 'Yes, of course,' she said smoothly, and took her book out of her handbag.

'No iPad?' he asked, sounding a bit surprised.

'Not for this. Pen and paper don't let you down and I can doodle and make notes to my heart's content.' She opened her book on a new page, her pen poised. 'Now, what were you thinking?'

'You tell me.'

'OK, well, a date would be a good start.'

'April,' he said. 'Or possibly March.'

'Could you be a little more specific?'

'Not immediately.'

'Right,' she said with a doubtful nod. 'Venue?'

'I'll have to get back to you on that.'

'Approximate number of guests?'

He shrugged.

'Food? Drink? Entertainment? Budget?' At his lack of response Abby arched an eyebrow. 'Let me guess—you'll be getting back to me on those too.'

'How could you tell?'

Stifling a sigh, she closed her book and put her pen down on top of it. 'Do you have any idea at all of what you'd like?'

'Not off the top of my head.'

This was all very strange, she thought, trying not to frown. Clients usually had at least *some* idea of what they wanted, but with Leo it was as if he'd only come up with the plan five minutes ago. And couldn't this initial approach have been done over the phone? 'Is it to be a surprise?'

'Why not?' he said, flashing her a quick smile that flipped her insides. 'It was to me.'

'What?' she asked, momentarily dazzled.

'Never mind.'

Hmm. 'Do you know what your parents like?'

'Not especially. But my mother's best friend will know who to contact and what they like. I'll let you have her details.'

'At last,' said Abby with a grin. 'Something you do know.'

'Makes a change, doesn't it?' he said, and she had the weirdest feeling that he wasn't just talking about the party.

'OK,' she said, shaking off the feeling, because anything other than the party was of no interest to her, and putting her pen and book back in her bag. 'I'll firm up the initial details with Jake and get a contract drafted.'

'Not Jake,' he said and she glanced up at him, somewhat surprised by the sharpness of his tone and the narrowing of his eyes.

'No?'

'Jake will be travelling. A lot. He won't have time to organise a party. You'll liaise with me.'

'Fine,' said Abby, although it wasn't fine at all because how the hell was she going to be able to keep her mind on the job when she was finding it so hard to resist the temptation to jump his bones? 'No problem. Just one thing, though…'

'What?'

'Won't it be awkward?'

'Won't what be awkward?' he said, looking at her as if he didn't know perfectly well what she was talking about.

'Well, you know, after what happened on Friday night.'

'I don't see why it should be,' he said dryly. 'It was just sex. Wasn't it?'

Abby swallowed. 'Right. Yes. Of course it was.'

'We should be able to be move past it, don't you think?'

Move past it. Yes. Definitely. Top idea, seeing as how he clearly hadn't been as bothered by the memory of it as she had. 'Oh, absolutely.'

'Great. So you'll do it?'

Of course she would. Apart from a Valentine's Day cocktail party and a couple of corporate events her diary was pretty much free until June, when the wedding season kicked in, so she'd be mad not to.

And actually, maybe moving past it would be easy and liaising with Leo *would* be all right because there probably wouldn't be much need to see him before the night of the party, whenever that was to be. Bar a couple of likely exceptions their contact could be kept entirely to email, text and occasionally the phone.

Relieved beyond belief that she'd found a way through the mess she was in, Abby beamed and said, 'I'd be delighted.'

The minute he saw Abby emerge from the door to the building that housed his office, Leo retreated from the window, sank into his chair, fell forward and started banging his head on the desk.

He was an idiot—bang. A bloody—bang —*bloody*— bang—fool. Why, oh, why hadn't he just cancelled the sodding meeting and to hell with cowardice, weakness and indecision? Quitting the banging, which had hurt more than he'd expected, Leo buried his head in his hands instead. Why hadn't he agreed that Jake would deal with the details? Why had he told her he'd be the one to liaise with her? She'd handed him the perfect solution to his problem on a plate and he'd rejected it without even considering it. Was he completely and utterly *insane*?

He'd told her that he didn't see why their recent history should be a problem but it was a problem. Of epic proportions. Because it was all he could think about and now, thanks to his spectacular brain fail, he was going to have to see her. Keep in touch with her. All the sodding time. To discuss ridiculous things like the colour of the napkins and whether to have fish or chicken when all he really wanted to discuss was where precisely she'd like him to ravish her.

And wasn't that a pointless discussion to be hoping for? He'd taken one look at her, in her knee-high brown suede boots, short suede skirt and a jumper of the softest pale blue, so very strokable and touchable and, yes, kissable, and he'd been a goner. He'd had to grip the edge of the desk to stop himself from reaching out and pulling her into his arms, while she'd sat there all cool and composed, a repeat of Friday night very much not going through her mind the way it was his.

He was a fool, but what was done was done and there was little he could do about it now without looking even more of an idiot. So he'd just have to grit his teeth, make sure he had an unshakable grip on his self-control and get on with it.

Deciding to start with bringing Jake up to speed just in case Abby ignored him and got in touch with his brother anyway, and wondering how the hell his life could have become so complicated within such a short period of time, Leo reached for his phone. He scrolled through the numbers until he found his brother's, hit the dial button and braced himself for a conversation he'd really rather not have.

'Jake?' he said when the call was answered.

'Hi, what's up?'

'Two things. First, we're throwing a surprise party for Mum and Dad's fortieth wedding anniversary.'

'Oka-a-ay,' said Jake after a beat. 'And second?'

'Second, remember the Madrid development which is running behind schedule and which I said I'd oversee?'

'Of course.'

'It's all yours.'

CHAPTER EIGHT

To: Leo Cartwright
From: Abby Summers
Subject: Cartwright ruby wedding anniversary party
Date: 16 December
Dear Leo
Following our meeting yesterday I'm writing to confirm that I'm thrilled to be entrusted with the organisation of your parents' ruby wedding anniversary. Please be assured that no effort will be spared in making this an event to remember.
Attached is a list of items for your consideration. I would be grateful if you could get back to me as soon as possible so I can make a start on the arrangements in the new year.
Kind regards, Abby

To: Abby Summers
From: Leo Cartwright
Subject: Re: Cartwright ruby wedding anniversary party
Date: 18 December
Dear Abby
I'm as thrilled as you are. Many thanks for sending over the document. I've now had a chance to look through all eight (?!) pages. My answers/queries are attached.
Best wishes, Leo

To: Leo Cartwright
From: Abby Summers

Subject: Party—queries
Date: 24 December
Dear Leo

Thank you for getting back to me so quickly. Believe me, eight pages is nothing when it comes to planning an event like this. Please find my answers to your queries below.

1. Re the venue, Barton Hall would be perfect, if you're sure it won't be an imposition. Three months isn't a lot of notice and suitable places can get booked up years in advance, so using your house is the ideal solution. I've had a quick glance at Google Earth and have identified a field that would be perfect for out-of-sight guest parking (outlined in red on the attached map—let me know if it's not suitable). As your parents will be familiar with the house it has the added benefit that fewer suspicions will be aroused.

2. I can, by all means, draw up a guest list, although it would be better if you did as you know your parents and their friends better than I do. I suggest enlisting the help of Jake and your mother's best friend.

3. No, you don't have to subtly quiz your parents about what they'd like if you don't want to, and you certainly don't have to video it. While this method can help me with the planning of surprise events, if you're not comfortable doing this the chances are that that element of the party may well be blown. Best not to risk it. With regards to decoration/tablecloths/napkins etc. we can stick to red and keep things tasteful.

4. Will you let Jake know he's to make the speech, or should I?

5. No, I don't think a black-tie dress code would be too 'stuffily formal'. After all this is quite an occasion.

6. You're right. People will probably bring gifts. A room and a member of staff dedicated to dealing with them will solve the problem of gifts/labels going astray.

7. Far from tight, the budget you've indicated is extremely generous and will make my job a lot easier/more fun. Not to mention giving the party a whole string of wow factors should you want them.

   As all the preliminary details have now been provided I've attached a breakdown of costs, and the contract. If everything is to your satisfaction, please print off two copies of each, sign and return to me for countersignature.
Abby
PS—If you were a fan of it, I'd wish you a Happy Christmas, but you aren't so I won't. Instead, I hope you enjoy the malt.

To: Abby Summers
From: Leo Cartwright
Subject: Christmas
Date: 24 December
But you are a fan of it, so Happy Christmas, Abby. Everything looks fine—contracts are in the post. Yes to wow factors. Sadly the malt never materialised but I should think I'll survive.
Leo

To: Leo Cartwright
From: Abby Summers
Subject: April 2
Date: 10 January

Hi, Leo

Happy New Year! (Surely you can't not be a fan of that?!) Just to let you know the following have been booked for April 2:

- · Caterers (please confirm menu choice)
- · Bar plus staff
- · 70s band
- · Florist
- · Heated marquee and associated furniture
- · Lighting specialist
- · Photographer
- · Magician
- · Pyrotechnician

If you could get a guest list to me by the end of the week I'll order the invitations on Monday.

Oh, and by the way, thank you so much for putting me in touch with Elsa Brightman. Did you know she was also your mother's maid of honour? Anyway, she's been brilliant with the details, and is an absolute mine of information. And not just with regards to your parents. Obviously discretion is my middle name and my lips are totally sealed, but let's just say, the summer you were twelve? The fortnight's grounding? I know what happened!

Abby x

To: Abby Summers
From: Leo Cartwright
Subject: Re: April 2
Date: 14 January

The summer I was twelve…? Hmm. Now let me think… Nope. Nothing springs to mind. But if, by any chance, you're referring to the night when the next-door neighbours' daughter's pyjama party which was being held in the tree house in the back garden was gatecrashed, it was all Jake's idea. Honest.

Guest list and menu selection attached.
Leo
PS—Happy New Year to you too.
PPS—Did you mean to sign off with a kiss?

To: Leo Cartwright
From: Abby Summers
Subject: Re: April 2
Date: 17 January
Absolutely. I regularly do so. All the time in fact. So rest assured it's not specific to you.
Abby xxxxx

To: Abby Summers
From: Leo Cartwright
Subject: Kissing
Date: 18 January
Shame.

To: Leo Cartwright
From: Abby Summers
Subject: Site visit
Date: 2 February
Hi, Leo
Thanks so much for arranging access to Barton Hall. Mrs Trimble was great about all of us swarming around taking measurements and photos—seriously, that housekeeper of yours has the patience of a saint. No obvious problems with the venue. On the contrary, it couldn't be more perfect.
The invitations went out last Friday. Please see the attached document, which will be kept updated with responses as they come in.

What do you think about letting off a bunch of red heart-shaped helium-filled balloons after the speeches?
Best wishes, Abby

To: Abby Summers
From: Leo Cartwright
Subject: Re: Site visit
Date: 2 February
Back to best wishes? Where are my kisses? And balloons? Why not?

To: Leo Cartwright
From: Abby Summers
Subject: Kisses
Date: 6 February
Kisses have to be rationed. I do have other clients, you know. How was your day-trip to Madrid?

To: Abby Summers
From: Leo Cartwright
Subject: Re: Kisses
Date: 6 February
Quick. Hectic. Unavoidable.
PS—Kisses rationed? Other clients? I'm devastated.
PPS—Whose idea was it to put together a forty-years-in-forty-seconds video of my parents' marriage? I like it.

To: Leo Cartwright
From: Abby Summers
Subject: Update
Date: 7 February
I'm sure you'll get over it :)
The video was my idea but Jake's the one who's taken it and is running with it. Should be fun to see what he comes up with!

Texts between Leo and Abby, February 15.

Another name to add to the guest list, I'm afraid. Blame Jake.

That seems to be a habit ;)

This time it's true. He's decided to bring a date.

Hah! I knew it! And yes, he's already sent over her contact details. No date for you?

No date.

Hang on, it's two o'clock in the morning. Don't you sleep???

I'm on a building site in Beijing. It's 10 a.m. What's your excuse?

Valentine's Day cocktail party. A late one.

Night off?

As if. Work.

Roses are red, violets are blue, I work too hard and Abby does too.

Very good. Not! When are you back? Plans are at the stage where it would be easier to go through them face-to-face.

Back the afternoon of March 1, but not free until the 5th. Unless you can do the evening of the first?

Given our tight timescale sooner rather than later would be good, so first is fine for me. Your office? What time?

Will need to eat.

Oblix. The Shard. 8 p.m.

Oooh, swanky. See you then. Goodnight, Shakespeare.

Goodnight.

CHAPTER NINE

'YOU KNOW, I STILL can't believe you cancelled on me,' said Gemma, who'd shown up at Abby's flat for a cup of tea at four and still hadn't left three hours later. 'Blowing out your best friend for a date. Huh. And whatever happened to Leo Cartwright with his emotional obstinacy not being the man for you?'

Abby eyed herself critically in the mirror that hung on the wall of her bedroom and ignored the quick leap of her pulse at the thought that in around an hour she'd see him again. 'He isn't the man for me,' she said, turning and twisting to check her bottom for a VPL. 'And this isn't a date. This is a business meeting.'

'Sure it is.

'It is.' After two weeks of pretty much constantly reminding herself of the facts, she could say it—and believe it—without wishing it were different because she didn't, of course, want it to be different.

Gemma glanced up from the magazine she was flicking through while lying stretched out on Abby's bed. 'Then why have you had your hair done?'

'Coincidence. It needed a cut.'

'This morning?'

'Why not?'

'You had it cut a fortnight ago.'

'So? Split ends have no concept of time.'

Gemma hmmed sceptically and went back to the magazine. 'Whatever. But I bet you don't normally wear that top for business meetings.'

'Why? What's wrong with it?'

'Nothing. It's fabulous. The colour really suits you and the sparkly bits are cool. But it's so low cut that all you have to do is lean forwards a bit and Leo will get an eyeful of cleavage.' She paused, then added, 'Actually, scrap that. You don't even need to lean forwards. And every time you move it'll shimmer and you'll be drawing attention to your boobs. Is that a coincidence too?'

Abby did a quick wiggle, then leaned forwards, and had to admit that Gemma had a point. About the coincidence thing too, because of course the timing of her haircut and her choice of outfit weren't a coincidence. Even though she knew perfectly well that this evening was nothing but business, she'd wanted to look as good as she could. As sexy as she could. Which was pathetic and pointless, but there it was.

She might not have seen Leo for a couple of months but that didn't mean she hadn't thought about him. She had. A lot. And not just in the strictly business sense.

It would probably have helped if she hadn't set up that Google alert so that every time he appeared anywhere online, a day or so later she'd find out about it.

After an initial flurry of alerts, from which she'd learnt that the brothers' company had been granted planning permission to develop a swathe of East London and that Jake had appeared at the opening of an art gallery in Mayfair, she'd told herself to delete it because these were things she didn't really need to know.

But every now and then up would pop a picture of Leo, inevitably looking all dark and smouldering and gorgeous, and she'd remember the things they'd done in bed together and she just couldn't bring herself to click on the delete button.

It also might have helped if she hadn't had such regular contact with Elsa Brightman, but there wasn't a lot she could have done about that. In the absence of any information coming direct from Leo's parents, and not a lot coming from either him or Jake, she was the best source Abby had.

The problem was that not only was she Leo's mother's best friend and maid of honour, she'd also been something of a semi-permanent fixture in the Cartwright household over the years, living close by as she did. And, heavens, did she have stories to tell about the boys. Stories she'd been delighted to share, with only the barest of prompts, and which Abby had lapped up.

She'd told herself that any information was useful to guarantee the success of the night, but, honestly, what need did she have for details about Leo's childhood? None. What relevance did what he'd got up to in his teens have? Again, none. All those girls he'd gone through at university and had occasionally brought home? She'd certainly had no valid reason to probe for details of *them*. And as for her delicate enquiries into his wedding day, which to her surprise had been very politely but very firmly rebuffed, well, those had no bearing on the proceedings whatsoever.

So when she encouraged Elsa to continue with her stories when she otherwise might have stopped it was nothing more than rampant curiosity and self-indulgence because she was intrigued and she simply couldn't get enough.

It was absurd, the hunger she had for information about him. Scarily absurd. And her inability to exert any sort of control over her thoughts was downright worrying.

As was the impatience with which she'd found herself waiting for his replies to her emails, texts and calls, the disappointment when a day went past with no word, and the excitement when he did get in touch. What that was all about she had no idea. She'd never been the type to wait and hope and obsess when it came to men, yet that was exactly what she'd become.

She'd also become reckless, irrational and careless, because how on earth could she have signed off one of her emails to him with a kiss? It didn't matter that Elsa had just told her about the night Leo and Jake had snuck up into that tree house to gatecrash the girls' pyjama party with torches and Frankenstein masks, and caused mayhem. It didn't matter that her heart had practically melted at the thought of it. The lapse in professionalism had been inexcusable.

As had been the subsequent shift in tone of their communication, which had definitely become more flirty. She couldn't ever recall bantering like that with a client, or using emoticons and exclamation marks with quite such abandon.

Yet deep down she'd loved it. Rather pathetically, it brightened her days. Gave her something to look forward to. Something to think about and, if she let herself, read far too much into, such as was he flirting back? If he was, why?

And that was why, like a poor, deluded, faintly desperate fool, she'd kept the dialogue going by asking ridiculous questions that resulted in her having to scour the internet for one hundred and twenty biodegradable red heart-shaped balloons and a helium pump, and making ridiculous suggestions, such as this totally unnecessary meeting.

With hindsight she shouldn't have done it. There was no need to meet. But she'd been working at that Valentine's Day cocktail party, surrounded by love and romance and smooching couples, and for a moment she'd felt so very, very lonely. She'd wanted nothing more than to be going home to someone. Someone to talk to, have a glass of wine with and snuggle up next to on the sofa.

Then he'd texted and told her he wasn't bringing a date to his parents' party, and quite suddenly, quite unexpectedly and quite desperately she'd wanted to see him.

But it had been a mistake because nothing would ever come of doing anything about her infatuation with Leo Cartwright. He wasn't the talking kind, even less the snuggling kind, and as he was unlikely to become any of that there was absolutely no point in continuing with it.

Glancing down at the top that had seemed such a good idea when she'd put it on, Abby sighed because Gemma was right. Apart from the heavy folder sitting on the kitchen table, nothing she'd done today in preparation for this evening was a coincidence, and for the sake of her sanity she needed to put a stop to it. 'I think I'd better change.'

Normally when he came back from a trip Leo was knackered. Normally all he wanted was to crash out and re-emerge only when he'd recovered. Not so tonight. Despite a ten-hour flight followed by an extremely frustrating extra hour circling over Heathrow he was feeling remarkably awake. Alert. Hyped, even. Whatever, sleep was the furthest thing from his mind.

Unlike Abby.

She'd barely been out of his thoughts over the last couple of months, and not just because she was organising this party. Try as he might—because what was the point when she clearly wasn't interested in him?—he couldn't stop thinking about the night they'd spent together. If he'd hoped that the memories would fade with time he'd been mistaken because if anything they'd sharpened and had very probably become exaggerated because surely the night couldn't have been *that* great.

What the hell he'd been thinking, sort of cyber-flirting with her, he had no idea. He ought to have been stamping out the flames not fanning them, but he just hadn't been able to help himself.

He'd been impressed by her efficiency and amused by her ideas. Teasing her about the kisses had been fun. And as for texting her about Jake's plus one when he knew perfectly well that his brother had already informed her of the change, well, he'd done that because it had been a while since he'd heard from her, and, standing there on the sixty-fifth floor of the skeleton building that shot into the sky leaving the chaotic mess of Beijing way below, he'd weirdly and unnervingly missed the contact, so it had simply been something he'd just had to do.

He couldn't explain any of it and wasn't entirely sure he wanted to be able to. All he knew was that he'd never been so distracted, never been so confused by his behaviour, and for a man who craved control, order and regularity, the absence of all three was a bit harrowing.

The one upside to the whole mad enterprise, he thought, rolling his glass of whisky between his hands as he sat at the table and waited for her to show up, was that getting through Christmas had been a breeze. With Abby's missives to look forward to and his own state of apparent mental collapse to deal with, he'd barely spared a moment's thought for Lisa and the humiliation she'd put him through, which was a huge relief because he was beginning to realise that five years was way too long to still be hung up on it.

But whatever he thought about Abby, whatever he wanted—and, as he glanced up and caught sight of her weaving her way through the tables, looking so beautiful that for a moment he forgot how to breathe, right now what he wanted involved forgetting dinner, grabbing her hand and carting her off to his place—it had to stop. This was business. Nothing more, nothing less, and if he didn't want to look like a pathetic drooling idiot he'd do well to remember it.

Pulling himself together and fixing a smile to his face, Leo got up. As she reached their table he glanced down at her outstretched hand for a moment and when he ignored it and gave her a quick kiss on the cheek instead it was hard to say who was more surprised.

'Hi,' she said, sounding a bit breathless and looking slightly flushed, but then she had been striding through the restaurant at quite a pace. He had no such excuse.

'Hello.'

He waited for her to sit down and then did the same. She thanked the waiter who'd pushed her chair in as she sat, and in response to his offer of a drink ordered a tequila. Then she stowed her handbag beneath her chair and fiddled with her napkin and all the while Leo couldn't take his eyes off her.

He didn't know why. It wasn't as if her outfit of black trousers and black polo neck was particularly revealing. And it wasn't as if she looked any different from the last time he'd seen her. Yet something about her was holding him captivated and rendering him unable to think, let alone speak, which was highly disturbing not least because he was now going to have to drum up some kind of conversation and once again his mind was blank.

'So how was your flight?' she said, sitting back and smiling at him and clearly having none of the trouble with basic functions that he was having.

'Long.'

'And China?'

'Productive.'

'What were you doing there?' she said, picking up the menu and opening it.

'Building a building.'

'What kind of building?'

'The tall kind.'

She frowned slightly and let out a tiny sigh—of exasperation?—and he told himself to get a grip and drum up some manners because he really ought to start contributing more to the conversation, and surely he could manage *that*.

'Actually,' he said, draining his drink and setting the glass on the table whereupon it was whisked away with the efficiency one would expect from one of the city's top restaurants, 'when it's finished it's going to be one of the biggest of its kind in Asia. It'll have a hundred and fifty floors and over three million square feet of retail, office and residential space. A twelve-storey underground car park, landscaped gardens and every kind of amenity you could possibly imagine. Construction is more or less half complete and while it hasn't been without its difficulties—' and, goodness, some of their partners had been tricky to handle '—things are looking good. The views from the upper floors are going to be breathtaking.'

He stopped and looked up to find Abby watching him with a smile that made his heart skip a beat. 'What?' he asked, frowning because since when had a smile ever done *that*?

'You love your job, don't you?'

'It's all consuming, stressful and frequently involves having to make near impossible deadlines so I couldn't do it to the extent I do if I didn't.'

'I suppose not.'

'Working with Jake helps.'

'You're very different.'

'That's probably why we work so well together.'

'So how did you get started?' she asked, once the waiter who'd materialised at their table had taken their order of scallops for Leo, smoked salmon for her and rare chateaubriand to follow, and then slipped away.

He shrugged and gave her the answer he gave most people. 'We were just two kids who happened to be in the right place at the right time and got lucky.'

Abby took a sip of her tequila and arched a sceptical eyebrow. 'Just like that?'

Remembering his decision to contribute to the conversation, Leo shot her a faint smile and said, 'No, not just like that, actually. I was just about to finish university and Jake was a couple of years off graduating when my mother gave us an inheritance she'd received so that we could buy our first flat. We did it up, sold it, bought two more with the proceeds. From there we kept multiplying and growing and then moving into developments overseas until we got where we are now. Jake has an excellent eye for detail and I have an affinity for numbers and it's a combination that seems to work.' He shifted in his seat and his smile turned wry. 'That's not to say we haven't had setbacks, especially in the beginning, and the state of the economy doesn't always co-incide with our plans, but we're doing OK.'

Abby grinned and glanced round at the expensive decor and the stunning views pointedly. 'More than OK, I'd say.'

'You're right. More than OK.'

The waiter appeared, produced a half-bottle of fino with a flourish and proceeded to fill first Abby's glass and then his.

Abby took a sip and hmmed in appreciation. 'This is nice,' she said, putting down her glass and twirling it by the stem. 'Unusual, but nice.'

Leo glanced down at her fingers and had an instant searing memory of those same fingers wrapped around a certain part of his anatomy. 'That's why I chose it,' he said a bit gruffly.

'So tell me about your parents.'

Leo cleared his throat and swiftly steered his mind back on track. 'Don't you know everything there is to know already? I thought Elsa Brightman was a mine of information.'

'She was,' Abby said with a nod, and he wondered with a brief stab of concern exactly how much information Elsa had revealed. 'But I'd like a son's perspective.'

'There's not a lot to say. They're just like most middle-class parents, I should think. Loyal. Unconditionally supportive. Totally non-judgmental when it comes to me and Jake. And while they've always wanted the best for us I think they're pretty bemused by what we've achieved. They're also immensely proud and refuse to take a penny from us, so with the party thing it feels good to be able to do something for them for a change.'

'I can imagine.'

'What about yours?'

'More or less the same. Bar the bemusement.'

'Do you have siblings?'

She nodded. 'Two older brothers. Charlie's a civil engineer and Steve's an oncologist.'

'And how did you get into event management?'

'By accident I suppose. I was all set to go to university to study politics, philosophy and economics, but during my year off I got a job with a catering company to earn some money.' She shrugged and smiled wistfully. 'And that was it really. I was hooked. Not on the catering, but on the whole events thing. I've always been pathologically organised and a bit of a perfectionist and my best friend, Gemma, who I worked with at the time in the catering company, suggested I go for it. I tossed up the pros and cons for a while, then jacked in uni and did an NVQ in event management instead.'

'What did your family think?'

Abby frowned and bit her lip for a second. 'Good question,' she said eventually. 'Outwardly they were fine with it. Just said I should do what I felt was right and that they'd be behind me whatever I chose to do. Inwardly, though, I have absolutely no idea.'

'How come?'

'They're not ones for emoting or expressing themselves much. On the one hand it drives me nuts—'

'Why?' interrupted Leo, curious because he considered not emoting and not expressing himself a perfectly good way of being. The best, in fact. It kept you safe, kept you strong. Invincible, unbreakable and always in control.

'Because no one ever says what they think or feel,' she said a bit heatedly, as if it was an argument she'd had many times before, 'and how can you possibly respond to anything if you don't know the facts? I can't stand having to second-guess all the time. It's so much better to have everything out there.' She stopped, thought for a moment, then shot him a quick smile. 'On the other it did give me the freedom to potentially screw up my future with no doubt about it whatsoever.'

'And you haven't screwed up.'

'Not yet. And I guess it has taught me self-reliance, independence of thought and to have courage in my convictions.'

'All good stuff.'

She looked at him thoughtfully. 'You'd think, wouldn't you?'

'You're very capable.'

'And is that bad?'

'Why on earth would that be bad?'

'No idea. But it's something I can't help,' she said and he got the feeling she was somehow apologising for it, although he couldn't imagine why. 'When I was sixteen my father had a heart attack. A bad one, although not fatal. My brothers were away at university and my mother sort of fell apart. It was left to me to keep things going for a couple of months. Make sure there was food in the house, bills were paid, doctors' appointments were kept, that kind of thing. Turned out I was good at it.'

'Would you ever considering expanding?'

'I'd love to but that would probably mean taking on someone else and handing over responsibility, and as a total control freak I don't know if I could do that.'

'Instead you work pretty much every hour of the day.'

'So do you.'

'True,' he said with a wry smile.

'So what do you do to relax?'

'I row.'

'In your gym?'

'On the river mainly.'

'That sounds nice,' she said. 'Peaceful.'

'It is. Very. When it isn't pelting.'

'Do you race?'

'Not since university. I don't have time to practise.'

'Do you miss it?'

'Only the winning.'

She tilted her head and studied him. 'And I bet you won a lot.'

'A bit,' he said, because admitting that he'd been a blue

and had won at Henley three years in a row would only come across as boasting. 'What about you?'

'I like winning too. Job pitches especially.'

'I meant, how do *you* relax?'

'Oh, I do the usual things when I have the time. Hang out with my friends. See my family.' She leaned forwards a little, her eyes shining and her smile broadening. 'Don't tell anyone but I also have a bit of an obsession with medical dramas on TV.'

'Medical dramas?' he echoed, faintly distracted by the way the gold glints in her hair caught the light of the candle.

She nodded. 'I can't get enough of them,' she said, and with effort he switched his focus to what she was saying. 'I think it's the sense of urgency and imminent chaos that appeals. The way things happen without warning. Failure is always a very real possibility even if four times out of five everything turns out fine and I guess that's the attraction. Chaos and failure aren't options for me, but nevertheless I do find them strangely addictive.'

'They're your vicarious kicks.'

'Exactly.'

'Did you know Jake's date for the party is the producer of *St Jude's*?'

Abby's jaw dropped and she nearly leapt out of her seat. 'Seriously?'

'Apparently so.'

'Someone's going to have to hold me back,' she said, and Leo's head instantly swam with images of him restraining her. With cuffs, scarves, belts, whatever came to hand, really, as long as she was naked and at his mercy.

Cursing his surprisingly active imagination, he shifted on his chair to ease the sudden pressure gripping in his lower body, and muttered, 'I'll warn her to be on the lookout.'

CHAPTER TEN

SO FAR, THOUGHT ABBY, smiling up at the waiter who was placing her starter of smoked salmon in front of her, so good. The evening was absolutely going as well as it could given the circumstances.

Admittedly it had been touch and go for a while at the beginning. She'd walked through the door and spotted Leo frowning down at the table, clearly deep in thought and looking tired and dishevelled but nevertheless so gorgeous that for a second she'd gone a bit dizzy.

For a moment she'd wished she'd rung him up and told him she couldn't make it. Then she'd contemplated turning around and leaving because suggesting they meet up had been reckless and foolish and she still had the smidgeon of a chance to rectify that.

But then he'd seen her and it had been way too late to back out. So she'd got a grip and told herself that her reaction was simply down to the initial shock of seeing him after so long. That she'd be fine once she'd got over it, and they'd got down to business.

Things had taken a slight turn for the worse when he'd kissed her cheek and she'd nearly passed out with the need to kiss him back, only properly. She'd looked up at him and had had the almost overwhelming urge to stroke away the lines of tiredness from his face and tell him that she'd missed him. But she'd got over that quickly enough.

By taking an unnecessarily long time to sit down and faff around with her handbag she'd more or less managed to haul herself under control, and now much to her surprise—and relief—she was enjoying herself.

Up until now they hadn't really engaged much in the way of general conversation, and so now she was finding it, well, kind of *nice* to be able to talk normally, without tension and without subtext.

As they chatted about everything from work to films to books, she discovered he was interesting. Dryly amusing and probably unintentionally entertaining.

Best of all, though, he was once again nothing more than a client, and therefore everything was absolutely back on track.

If he'd known what torture dinner was going to be Leo would have suggested meeting Abby somewhere else entirely. Like a supermarket. A car park. His office. Hers. Anywhere that wasn't softly lit and encouraged seduction.

He'd known that after the long flight he'd be hungry for good food and he'd assumed a restaurant would be safe enough, but it wasn't because at no point had he taken into consideration the fact that once the food arrived he'd be unable to resist the temptation to watch her. As she ate, as she drank, as she talked and as she moved.

He couldn't help it. She was so expressive, her movements so fluid and graceful as she talked about the events she'd organised and how, by way of a recommendation, she'd come to work for them.

And then there was the way she'd sighed over the food. With every tiny sigh he'd itched to sweep the table aside and tumble her to the floor, and once that thought had entered his head kissing her, undressing her and touching her was all he could think about. He was finding it so hard to concentrate on what she was saying with the images that were spinning through his head that he'd had to resort to non-committal hmms and vague agreement or disagreement depending on her expression.

He watched her put down her coffee cup, turning it so that the handle sat exactly at ninety degrees, and he even found *that* arousing, which meant that he was in a bad, *bad* way.

'So we should talk about the party,' she said, and for a split second he was about to ask, Party? What party? before sense returned and in the nick of time he remembered the whole original point of this evening.

'That's what we're here for,' he said, astonishingly sounding as if he actually meant it.

'Yes, it is, isn't it?' she said, and then with the help of a folder that she extracted from her bag, placed on the table and started flicking through, proceeded to outline exactly what was planned and how it was all going to work.

He watched her talk, her face growing more and more animated as she shared the details, and words like 'table plan', 'soaking of the oasis'—which would have baffled him even if his brain *had* been running at one hundred per cent—and 'setting up' danced around him, barely filtering into his head because if he wanted to know more he could presumably appropriate the folder and, besides, he was enjoying listening to her far too much to concentrate on the actual details.

'As a decoy,' he heard her say through the fog in his head and his focus sharpened a fraction because he'd actually been wondering about this, 'I thought, seeing as how your parents are such opera buffs, you could invite them to a black-tie recital at Barton Hall. A charity thing. Jake would bring them, and then, *ta-da*, surprise.'

'Good plan,' he murmured before zoning out again as she moved on to timings and speeches and the design for the firework display.

'And then I thought,' she said, tilting her head and narrowing those incredible blue eyes a little, 'how about flying a dozen camels over from Dubai and holding races down the drive, with jockeys and betting and everything? Your parents could present the trophies.'

'Sounds great,' he murmured, vaguely wondering how unusual the combination of her hair and eye colour was because he didn't think he'd ever come across it before.

'Leo.'

At the sharpness of her voice he blinked and gave himself a quick shake. 'What?'

'Have you been listening to a word I've been saying?'

'Of course I have.'

'What's the plan for the decoy?'

'An opera recital.'

'Timings for the drinks?'

'I'll take a look at the folder.'

'And the camels?'

'Camels?' he asked with a frown as he thought, *damn, how on earth did camels fit in?* and thereby totally gave himself away.

'I thought not,' she said, shaking her head in disappointment, her smile gone. 'Look, if you don't care about any of this, if you're not particularly interested, all you have to do is say.'

He did care and he was interested. In the party, a lot. In her, even more.

And frankly he'd had enough. Of the confusion, the lack of concentration, the constant tension inside him. Of everything about her that had turned his life upside down since the moment they'd met, in fact.

So to hell with business. And to hell with what she thought about him. He couldn't contain it any longer, because if he did he feared he might actually go mad.

Hadn't she said it was better to put the facts 'out there'? That second-guessing was a waste of time? Well, for once he was going to put how he felt 'out there', and she could do what she liked with it.

'Want to know why I was distracted?' he asked, he

thought coolly enough but his voice must have held an edge because she went very still.

'I'm not sure,' she said, her breath catching and her gaze fixed on his. 'Do I?'

'I'll tell you anyway.'

'OK.'

'Your mouth moves and all I can think of are the amazingly clever things you can do with it. I look at your hands and all I can remember is how they felt on me. I listen to your voice and all I can hear is you telling me to go harder, deeper, faster. The memory of us together won't go away, Abby, and it's undoing me.'

For the longest time she didn't say anything. But the pulse at the base of her neck was hammering like crazy, her breathing was rapid and shallow and her cheeks flushed deep.

'I thought what happened wasn't going to be a problem,' she said and her voice was husky.

'So did I.'

'Yet it clearly is.'

'I overestimated the strength of my willpower because I can't stop thinking about you. That night. The things we did.' He stopped. Tilted his head and held her gaze. 'Has it crossed your mind *even once*?'

She looked at him steadily, her eyes clear and unguarded, and after a beat said, 'It's on my mind pretty much constantly.'

At her admission his brain reeled, his pulse raced and his one overriding thought was that as soon as they were done here he was taking her home and keeping her there until the desire and the tension had gone.

Until she added, 'But that doesn't mean I'm planning to do anything about it,' and he reeled a bit more, the disappointment slamming through him sudden and excoriating.

'What?' he asked, his voice rough.

'You know I don't mix business and pleasure.'

'Why not?'

'Experience.'

'What happened?'

'I once had a client who thought that sleeping with me entitled him to a one-hundred-per-cent discount. When I said no, that was it. No more client, but four months of bad-mouthing that meant no work for me until it fizzled out and everyone moved on.'

'I won't ask you for a discount.'

She eyed him coolly. 'You won't get the chance.'

'You want me.'

'Maybe I do, but I can resist.'

'Liaise with Jake instead of me over this party and you don't have to.'

'It's still your name on the contract.'

'A technicality.'

'But a crucial one.'

She was stubborn, and while half of him admired her for it, the other half damned it to hell. 'Is there anything I can say to change your mind?'

'Not a thing.'

'You're really not going to budge?'

'Not even a millimetre.'

He took in the set of her jaw, the challenge in her eyes and realised that this wasn't a battle he'd be winning. Not here and now, at least.

And that was fine because now he knew that she wanted him as much as he wanted her he could wait. He only had to hold out a few more weeks and he could easily manage that. In the meantime he'd perhaps spend the weeks wearing down her resistance so that by the time the party was over she'd be begging for him to take her to bed, and his track record of avoiding rejection would once again be blemish-free.

'OK,' he said with a casual shrug and an even more casual smile that gave away nothing of his thoughts. 'Then I'd better get the bill.'

* * *

The ease with which Leo had let the whole business/pleasure thing go had been surprising, but as Abby prepared for bed later that night she certainly wasn't complaining. He'd never know how close she'd come to giving in. How tempted she'd been to hurl aside the table and launch herself at him and to hell with the principle that had helped keep her and her business on the straight and narrow.

So much for thinking that everything was fine. She should have known that things would implode. She should have been prepared for it.

But really, how could she have been? She'd never *ever* have imagined that Leo-tighter-than-a-clam-Cartwright would have actually put what he was thinking into words. Even once he *had*, she'd struggled to believe what she was hearing.

He'd badly rocked her resolve. He'd certainly rocked her thought processes because maybe she shouldn't have told him that she thought about him and that night all the time. Maybe it would have been better to deny it and pretend that the chemistry that arced between them wasn't an issue.

But then again, as she'd told him, she'd never believed in not saying what she thought and what she felt when the need arose, and the need had definitely arisen then because her nerves had been shredded.

So no, she'd done the right thing, she thought, throwing back the duvet and climbing into bed.

It had been much better to acknowledge that there was something between them because once she'd done that she'd been able to deal with it. And she had. Successfully. It had been a close-run thing, and if Leo had pushed even a little bit further she might have relented, but her sense of self-preservation was still intact because somehow—thankfully—she'd convinced him to stop.

Now all that remained was for her to do the same about

the sweet, aching tension in her muscles and the hot throbbing between her legs and everything would be back under control.

Given how badly he'd been sleeping and how much effort he'd expended—fruitlessly—on wondering how he could wear away Abby's obstinate resistance without drawing attention to what he was doing, the last thing Leo felt like was meeting up with his brother to be introduced to his new date.

For one thing, ever since their parents' anniversary party had come into being things had been a bit tense between them. Shortly after Leo had informed his brother of the fact that he'd be spending much of his time in Madrid, they'd met up for a beer and within five minutes of sitting down Jake had begun interrogating him with a tenacity that Leo normally admired but then had had him gritting his teeth.

Despite Leo's lack of input and his icy glares Jake hadn't let up, prodding, dropping Abby's name into the conversation at every possible opportunity and smiling knowingly, until Leo had slammed his glass down on the table, shot him a look that could have frozen hell and told him to shut up. Which seemed to have done the trick because Jake had backed off and stayed backed off ever since.

For another, spending a couple of hours watching the latest in a long line of women moon over his brother and knowing that the relationship would last only marginally longer than his did, wasn't his idea of fun.

He wasn't envious, as Jake was so fond of suggesting. He didn't do envy, and, besides, what was there to be envious of? He just didn't particularly enjoy being a gooseberry, and he didn't particularly enjoy having to bite his tongue so that he didn't tell whoever was wrapped round his brother at the time not to bother, that was all.

But then he'd considered the alternative, which was trying not to fantasise about Abby and what he was going to do with her the minute the party was over, a battle he inevitably ended up losing, and he'd settled for the option that was marginally less unappealing.

And that was how he'd come to be at The Cross and Sceptre halfway through his second pint and trying to stifle a yawn.

It wasn't that Caroline Adams wasn't charming. She was. She was attractive, amusing and had dozens of entertaining stories about the things that had happened on the set of *St Jude's*. He could see why Jake was, however temporarily, captivated. But he was knackered and keen to get home to work on his strategy for dealing with Abby.

Which was why he was only paying the barest attention to what Caroline was saying, until she happened to mention that they were a month or so away from filming the thousandth episode of the show that Abby loved so much and suddenly he was on full alert.

Light bulbs were flashing in his head left, right and centre, and the strategy that had proved so frustratingly elusive recently became blindingly clear.

Adrenalin pumping, he put his glass on the table with such force that both Jake and Caroline jumped. 'Well, now, that sounds like something to celebrate,' he said, obviously sounding more enthused than he had all evening if the way they were staring at him in surprise was anything to go by.

'It does, doesn't it?' said Caroline with a bright smile.

'Need an event planner?'

'Do you know one?'

Ignoring his brother's smug smile, Leo kept his gaze pinned to the woman who might well turn Abby to putty in his hands, and said, 'As it just so happens, I do.'

As Abby had hoped, everything was totally back under control, until about a week after that dinner, when Leo rang to say that he'd heard about some work she might be interested in and if she could spare a day midweek to follow it up with him it would be worth her while.

She couldn't really spare a day midweek but neither could she refuse the possibility of work—the memory of those four months of absolutely nothing in the diary had never completely faded—so on Thursday morning, in response to the peal of the doorbell, Abby found herself heading down the stairs with a spring in her step and a buzz of excitement that had nothing to do with seeing Leo again and everything to do with the prospect of a job.

The tiny lurch that her heart gave when she opened the door and saw him standing on the step, looking all tall, dark and serious, was as a result of nearly tripping up on a wrinkle in the hall carpet. The quick tightening of her stomach had to be hunger because for the first time in years she hadn't quite got round to breakfast. The sudden dryness of her mouth was, naturally, down to too much coffee and not enough water.

'Good morning,' said Leo, giving her a barely there smile.

'Is it? For me it's a bit too early to tell.'

The smile deepened into a grin as he backed off the step and waited for her to lock her front door before walking beside her to the car.

'Ready to go?' he asked, holding open the passenger door for her.

'Not really,' said Abby, because he'd been unnervingly vague about the details, 'but I intend to remedy that as soon as we're on our way.'

Taking great care not to brush against him, she slid into the car and wondered how the hell she was going to handle who knew how long a journey with him in such close proximity. All that presence, that masculinity filling what was really a very small, very confined space.

She had to focus, she thought, doing up her seat belt and sitting back against the soft leather while staring ahead in an effort to not watch Leo do the same. Concentrate on business. Not on his hands on the steering wheel or his hard-muscled, jean-clad thighs so close that touching them would be almost accidental…

Business, she told herself, snapping her gaze back to where it should be, that was, the windscreen. That was the thing.

'Are you going to tell me where we're going?' she asked as he pulled away from the kerb, drove down the road and smoothly slipped into the heavy rush-hour traffic.

'I wasn't planning on it.'

'Why not?'

'It's a surprise.'

Abby twisted round a bit and stared at him. She couldn't help it, and it did give her a lovely view of his profile. 'A surprise?'

'That's right.'

'As a rule event planners aren't great fans of surprises. We're good at organising them, lousy at being on the receiving end of them, especially when the latter happens slap bang in the middle of the former.'

'I think you'll like this one.'

She doubted it. She doubted it very much, and now she wished she'd quizzed him a bit harder when he'd first suggested this trip, wished she hadn't been quite so dizzily distracted by the sound of his voice. 'You said it was about work.'

'That's right. There's a party to be organised.'

'What for?'

'You'll see.'

Abby dropped her gaze to the faint smile that was tugging at his lips, and frowned. 'Why do I get the feeling that you're pleased with yourself?'

'Because I am.'

And just like that her temper sparked because she was

tired, frustrated and tense, her career was not his plaything and actually there was nothing remotely amusing about any of this. 'OK, look, Leo. I get that this is, for some reason, tickling you pink, and you think you're being really clever and mysterious by being so secretive, but consider my point of view for a moment. I'm heading to a business meeting about which I know absolutely nothing. I don't know who the client is. I've had no chance to prepare or to do any research. I don't like it. I don't feel comfortable. And you're not playing fair.'

'Maybe not but you'll be fine. You can organise a party standing on your head with your eyes closed.' He shot her a quick searing glance that did nothing to calm the flurry of nerves that were churning up her stomach. 'And besides, I should think you know pretty much everything there is to know about the client.'

'I do?'

'Yup.'

That was some small comfort, she supposed, but still... 'How would you feel if the roles were reversed?'

'One hundred per cent confident in my ability.'

'Sure you would.'

'I'd also trust me.'

'Easy for you to say. You know you. I don't.'

'I'd trust you.'

'Why?'

'You've never given me cause not to.'

'Neither have I given you much cause *to* trust me. Nor you me.'

There was a pause and then he said with a conviction she'd never heard from him before, 'Abby, all you need to know is that if I say it'll be fine, it will be.'

'Are you really not going to tell me?'

'Nope.'

And that was when she gave up because she could hardly

force it out of him, could she? And as she wasn't willing to throw herself from a moving vehicle, what else could she do but just as he suggested and trust him?

'Then it seems I have little choice,' she said a bit grumpily.

'If it helps we'll be there in around an hour.'

'Do you mind if I catch up on some work en route?'

'Not at all.'

And that was what she did. She took out her iPad, blocked Leo from her thoughts, and as they crossed the river and headed north through the city she sent emails, added appointments to her diary and made lists.

She was so engrossed she barely noticed the car slowing an hour or so later. It was only when Leo cut the engine that she glanced up and saw that they'd stopped in front of a barrier that kept people out of what looked like a huge industrial estate.

'What's going on?' she asked, looking around and wondering whether she'd been right to put her trust in him after all because they appeared to be in the middle of nowhere and it was deserted.

'We're here.'

'Where's here?' she asked, and thought that she really should have paid more attention to where they were heading.

'They're expecting you,' he said, undoing her seat belt, then leaning across her, opening her door and practically pushing her out in the direction of the booth. 'Give me a call when you're done. Have fun.'

CHAPTER ELEVEN

THREE HOURS LATER Abby was back at the barrier, still buzzing, still reeling, still unable to believe that she'd just had a tour of the set of her favourite TV show, had met some of the cast and had all but got the job of planning a party to celebrate a thousand episodes.

As Thursday mornings went, this one had been a corker.

And it was all down to lovely, lovely Leo.

Caroline—fabulous producer and practically her new best friend—had told her about the drink. She'd told her about how he'd recommended her, and how he'd fixed up not just the meeting but also the tour, and as a result Abby was now filled with nothing but warm, melty, gooey thoughts for him.

Setting up a meeting was one thing, but requesting a tour surely went beyond making a simple professional recommendation, didn't it? It meant that he'd remembered her love of the programme. It meant that he'd done something for her that he knew she'd enjoy.

Which meant...what exactly? Something? Nothing? What?

With her brain going into overdrive as she tried to work it out Abby sent Leo a quick text to tell him she was done, and leaned against the booth to wait.

Would she be reading too much into this morning if she considered the possibility that maybe their relationship was slipping into something a bit more...well, *personal*?

Could she even begin to wonder whether, as unbelievable and contrary to her previous experience as it seemed, he might actually be changing in his approach to emotion?

After all, his declaration of his feelings in the restaurant and now this would suggest he was. A bit. Maybe. And if he *was* beginning to open up and their relationship *was* shifting, then what was she going to do about it? What did she *want* to do about it?

Hmm.

Perhaps she was being a bit over the top with the whole business/pleasure mixing thing, she thought, frowning down at the ground and biting her lip. Surely her business wouldn't go down the tubes if she broke her rule just this once? Things were very different today from what they had been seven years ago. She was on a far firmer footing business-wise, and she was no longer naïve when it came to men.

Besides, Leo wasn't the kind of man who'd use what went on between them for his own ends. He hadn't yet, and she could think of no reason why he would. He wouldn't need to.

So maybe disaster wouldn't strike if she gave into the desire that had, if she was being honest, been eating her up inside and driving her totally nuts. It might even be fun. It would certainly be hot...

And right now, she thought, her heart hammering and the possibilities of an affair racing through her head as she watched his car come round the corner and pull up right in front of her, so was she.

Leo watched Abby approach his car as if she were floating on air, her eyes shining, her cheeks pink and her smile wide, and satisfaction shot through him.

Oh, yes, fixing up this trip had been a stroke of genius. A stroke of bloody genius. He'd thought she'd love it, and it seemed as though he'd been right. And as a result, she was his. Absolutely and without doubt.

Or she would be before very long, he amended, climbing out and striding round to the passenger side to open the door for her, because those light bulbs that had started flashing a week ago in the pub hadn't stopped and he'd come up with an offensive that couldn't possibly fail.

Once they got back to London he was planning to capitalise on the success of this morning by inviting her out to a dinner designed to seduce. Then there'd be another and another, and possibly another. He'd intersperse the dinners with a picnic. The theatre. The Boat Race. And whatever else he could think of.

She wouldn't have time to question or doubt or wonder what he was doing. Her head would be too busy spinning with the charm he'd be hitting her with. Or trying to, at least, because he had to admit that therein lay the only flaw to an otherwise perfect plan. Not that it was a major flaw. No. He was, perhaps, a little rusty on the charm front, but he used to have gallons of the stuff, and surely it couldn't be *that* hard to dust it off and put it into practice.

'Hi,' she said, giving him a dazzling smile as she slid into the passenger seat.

'Hi,' he replied, duly dazzled as he shut her door, made his way round to his side, got in.

She was peering at the dashboard. 'Do you have air conditioning in this thing?'

'This *thing*,' said Leo, a bit bemused by the effect that a mere smile could have on him, 'can do nought to a hundred in six point eight seconds. It has a V12 engine, five hundred and forty-seven horsepower, and every gadget known to car manufacturing. Of course it has air conditioning.'

Abby flashed him another blinding smile. 'Great. Would you mind switching it on?'

'Not at all,' he muttered, pressing a button and switching the temperature to low because now he thought about it it was kind of warm in here.

'Thanks.'

He fired up the engine and then they were on their way. 'So how did it go?'

'It was completely and utterly amazing,' she said, the delight in her voice so obvious it made him smile. 'I don't think I'll be coming down off the high for days.'

'I told you to trust me, didn't I?'

'You did.'

'Was it worth it?'

Abby flashed him a grin. 'What do you think?'

'The job?'

'In the bag.'

'Well done,' he said, and told himself that whatever it was that had just stabbed him in the chest was hunger because it couldn't possibly be pride. Definitely hunger. He was ravenous.

'Thanks. Although I'm not sure how much of it was down to me and how much of it was Caroline wanting to stay in Jake's good books.'

'Don't be modest,' said Leo, knowing that wanting to stay in Jake's good books was a complete waste of time. 'You're brilliant at what you do.'

'Thank you.'

'Tell me more about this morning.'

'Are you sure? Because once I start I might not be able to stop.'

'We have an hour to kill,' he said. 'So I say, go for it.'

She shifted and twisted round a bit and even though he had to keep his eyes on the road he could feel hers on him. Could feel the heat of her gaze right down to his bones.

'Well,' she said, her voice brimming with enthusiasm, 'first of all I had the set tour, which was absolutely fascinating. You know parts of it are actually like a proper hospital. I bet if push came to shove they could carry out real operations there.'

'Would you want to risk it?'

'I would if Joe Hamilton was the doctor on duty.'

'Joe Hamilton?' said Leo, thinking, as his gaze flickered

from the road to her for a second, that he didn't like the look of adoration on her face one little bit.

'Cardiac surgeon. Brilliant. Gorgeous. Arrogant. Big hit with the women but a total bastard, naturally. I saw him having a sneaky cigarette behind a trailer. We chatted for a bit and it was dreamy,' she added with a sigh.

Leo hmmed and frowned and told himself that he couldn't possibly be jealous of this Joe Hamilton person because being jealous of a fictional character was just plain mad.

'Then what?' he prompted when the silence stretched for a bit too long and it occurred to him that she might well have drifted off into a daydream about the brilliant, gorgeous cardiac surgeon.

'Oh. Well, then I got to see some actual filming, which is of course far less glamorous and far harder work than you might think as a viewer. And when it was time to stop I had lunch with the cast and crew.'

'Fun?'

'Brilliant. The stories they have. You wouldn't believe half of them... So, anyway, what about you? What did you do while I was living it up with the stars?'

'I checked out a site nearby for possible development.'

'Interesting?'

'Very.'

'So a good day had by all, then?'

'It would seem so.'

And if things went the way he hoped it was only going to get better.

Abby couldn't remember the last time an hour had passed so quickly or conversation had been so effortless. They'd told each other more about their mornings, and then moved on to other, more general things. She'd asked him about rowing and he'd invited her to the Boat Race. A casual invitation, sure, but that hadn't stopped her holding it close and melting a little bit more inside.

She couldn't remember ever wanting someone so much, quite so desperately either, but then she'd never come across anyone like Leo before.

Where he'd got the reputation for being cold, ruthless and forbidding she had no idea because when the man put his mind to it he could be charming. Very charming indeed. Who'd have thought that he'd turn out to have a sense of humour, albeit an extremely dry one? Who'd have thought he'd actually be able to crack jokes?

Her immunity to it, to him, was now non-existent, and she'd lost count of the number of times she'd had to bite her tongue to stop herself demanding he drive her to the nearest hotel. And it didn't even matter, because now she'd decided to embark on a fling, relationship, whatever with him, she didn't need to be immune. She didn't need to resist him any longer.

All she needed to do was tell him. And wasn't now, when they'd arrived back at her house and were within spitting distance of privacy and a bed, the perfect time?

'Thank you, Leo,' she said, unclipping her seat belt and twisting round to face him, her heart pounding so hard she was in danger of cracking a rib.

'What for?'

'Today. Setting up the meeting. And the tour.'

'No problem.'

She smiled. 'It was thoughtful.'

There was a moment's silence, then he frowned. 'Thoughtful?'

'It's the first time that anyone's set anything up for me in as long as I can remember.'

'What do you mean?'

'When you do what I do, whenever there's a wedding or a party or whatever—and I don't mean work, I mean when it comes to friends—you end up being asked to organise it. And it's fine. It really is. I love it. It's just that every now and then it would be nice to go to something that I haven't had to organise. Like today. It was lovely.'

You're lovely, she thought, although that was something she'd be keeping to herself for now because it was so unbelievably sentimental if she did tell him she'd only sound like a soppy fool. Instead she let her gaze drift over his face. She saw heat in his eyes and tension in his jaw. She heard the tiny hitch of his breath and it drew her attention to his mouth.

Then it was she who was being drawn to him because almost as if she had no control over herself she was slowly moving forwards, closer and closer, until her mouth was a centimetre from his and she could sense the restraint he was exerting over himself, not moving a muscle.

And for a split second, a moment before their mouths met, Abby hesitated. Once she did this there'd be no going back, so was she one hundred per cent sure she wanted to?

She was, oh, how she was…

'Do it,' he said so softly she almost didn't hear him.

'Do what?'

'Kiss me.'

'Is that what you think I'm thinking of doing?' she murmured teasingly.

'Yes.'

'Can't imagine why.'

His gaze held hers. Their breaths mingled, and she was nearly passing out with anticipation. 'You want to. You know you do. I know you do. So do it. Out of gratitude, if nothing else.'

What?

Abby went still. 'Out of gratitude?' she said, drawing back and frowning at him, the feelings of loveliness and anticipation evaporating beneath a whirl of confusion. 'Why would I kiss you out of gratitude?'

'Because you are. Grateful, I mean. Aren't you?' He smiled faintly. Warmly. With satisfaction.

In triumph?

'So you might as well give in, Abby,' he said, and just like that her dreamy bubble burst and everything about today became blindingly and horribly clear.

By organising the meeting and the set tour Leo hadn't been being thoughtful. He hadn't been being lovely.

He'd been manipulating her. And why? Well, to make her break her work/pleasure rule and get into her knickers, of course. Why else?

How *could* she have been such a fool?

Hadn't she thought he'd given in remarkably easily when she'd turned him down at dinner a week ago? Hadn't she congratulated herself on a job well done? She should have analysed it more. Should have asked herself the questions such an end to the night should have thrown up.

And she was *such* an idiot for assuming he'd changed. Such a bloody idiot. Or course he wouldn't have changed. He was a man. There she'd been thinking that there was something going on between them, that things were maybe *developing*, and all he'd been doing was manoeuvring her into bed.

Everything he'd said today had been planned. Designed. Calculated. He hadn't suddenly decided to open up to her. He hadn't suddenly embraced the idea of expressing his feelings, his innermost thoughts. And he never would.

Yet she'd been imagining a *relationship* with him. Had she gone truly insane? Would she *never* learn? After all she wasn't even dateable, was she? Not after the night she'd slept with him. Not now. Maybe not ever again.

Why would he do something nice, something *thoughtful*, for her anyway? They hardly knew each other. She was nothing more than a challenge to be won, and she'd been so blindsided by the strength of their chemistry, the charm, her fledgling feelings, which with hindsight she should have nipped in the bud way back, she just hadn't seen it coming.

Well, whatever, she thought, the hurt and humiliation shooting through her congealing into something hard and cold in her stomach. She saw it now. She saw it all. The tiny part of her that was flattered that he wanted her so much could forget it. His behaviour sucked. He wasn't the man she'd thought he was. He was a louse. And as for her, there weren't words to describe what an idiotic fool she'd been. Talk about dumbing down. She hadn't even needed to *try*.

'On second thoughts,' she said coolly, 'forget the kiss.'

Leo's smile faded and he looked genuinely perplexed, as well he might, because he must have thought he had her right where he wanted her. 'Forget it?'

'I'm grateful, but I'm not *that* grateful.'

He frowned. 'I don't get it.'

'Don't you?' she said, arching an eyebrow, her tone just this side of scathing because that she'd been such a fool hurt. Badly. 'Really? Well, why don't I put you straight? I know what you're doing, Leo.'

'What's that?'

'Today. The meeting. The tour. The charm. The invitation to the Boat Race. It's all been about buttering me up.'

Something flickered in the depths of his eyes, and his fingers tightened on the steering wheel and if she'd had any last, lingering hope that she'd got it wrong, that he was interested in her and not just because of the heat they generated in bed, it evaporated.

'What *I* don't get,' she said, using the stab of pain to fuel her words instead of rip her apart, 'is why you would do something like that. Why you would go to such lengths just to get me back into bed.' She kept her gaze fixed to his but it was hard when it was so impossible to work out what was going on in that warped head of his. 'And why would you so completely disrespect my decision to keep work and fun separate? Does what I want matter so little compared with what you want? Why have you singled me out? What's so important about me?' She broke off to give him a chance to answer any one of those questions, but of course he didn't, so she said as much for her benefit as his, 'You know, my time is too valuable to waste playing such ridiculous games and I'd have thought yours was too. So you know what? Enough of this. It stops now. I'll see you at the party, Leo, and not a moment before.'

And how she did it she'd never know with the way her whole body was shaking, but she got out of the car, walked up to her front door and she didn't look back once.

It was only when Abby closed her front door behind her and disappeared from view that the restraint Leo had been employing snapped, and, swearing violently, he thumped the steering wheel.

How had things gone so badly wrong? How had he managed to ruin what had been a near-perfect moment? Everything had been going so well. *So* well. He'd had her practically in the palm of his hand. She'd been on the verge of giving in, kissing him, and he'd been burning up with anticipation, dizzy with desire. He'd been so close to achieving what he wanted and giving her what he knew she wanted.

And then—snap—he'd screwed it up.

It had been the 'thoughtful' thing that had done it, he thought darkly, wishing he could rewind time and do the last ten minutes again. That she'd so totally misread the situation had made him feel uncomfortable. Somehow traitorous. And oddly guilty.

Not liking or understanding any of that he'd needed to get things back on track, put what was happening back into perspective, and that was why he'd gone for the gratitude angle.

But what a mistake that had been because he'd underestimated Abby. He'd never considered that she might see his plan for what it was, but he should have because unlike him she was no fool.

He'd never considered the consequences of her seeing through him either, but if he had he'd have assumed he'd have felt annoyed. Frustrated, perhaps.

Instead he felt like a complete and utter heel.

Leo ran his hands through his hair and forced himself to unclench his jaw before it shattered. He should have said something when she'd launched all those questions at him. In this instance silence had not been an effective weapon. It had simply proven his guilt.

But what could he have said when she'd been right on practically every count?

Her words ricocheted around his brain all over again and he grimaced in, yes, *shame*, because what right did he have to so completely disrespect her wishes? None. Was what he wanted more important than what she wanted? Of course not.

He'd been acting like a jerk. Envious of and frustrated by her strength of will when his was non-existent, and completely overwhelmed by the attraction, the desire he had for her.

But that was all it was, he reassured himself, as he struggled for calm. Desire. It would fade. Eventually. It always did. He didn't know why he'd singled her out. There wasn't anything special about her. And their time *was* too precious to waste.

So that would be it, he thought, pulling himself together and gunning the engine. No more obsessing. No more planning. And no more games. He'd be backing right off.

The reasons Leo had rescheduled all his appointments for the three days that ran up to party night, therefore, were purely of a practical nature.

For one thing the event was taking place at his house. If there were any questions about anything it would be better and quicker if he was on hand to answer them. For another, as he'd never really thought about the preparations of any event he'd ever attended, he'd like to see what was going on, how things were done, and, in this case, where, exactly, his money was being spent. He wanted to make sure no damage was done to the furniture. See that no one ran off with the silver. That sort of thing. He might even be able to help.

Besides, it had been a while since he'd been down here, and he'd kind of forgotten why he'd bought the house in the first place. It would be good to reconnect with the building and figure out what he was going to do with it.

If the need arose, he could easily work from here. And relax, because it was peaceful out here, and on the bank of the lake was a boathouse, which contained at least two skiffs and half a dozen oars.

His reasons for coming had nothing to do with wanting to see Abby, of course. Absolutely nothing at all. She'd told him in no uncertain terms to back off and leave her alone, and that was exactly what he'd done.

Bar replying to a couple of emails she'd sent he hadn't been in touch, and that had been absolutely fine. He hadn't missed the contact in the slightest. He hadn't missed *her* in the slightest. The last fortnight had been terrific. Not as busy as he'd have liked work-wise, but, hey, he'd sculled so many miles along the Thames he could have gone to Holland and back. Twice. And taking his parents to the Boat Race had been fun. *Huge* fun.

He had to admit, though, that staying away from Abby hadn't been easy. His conscience had kicked in with full force practically the minute he'd arrived at his office after dropping her home, and had then set about hammering him with wave upon wave of guilt at the way he'd behaved. Guilt that time had only increased and only a grovelling apology might assuage.

But how could he deliver an apology when she was undoubtedly not in the frame of mind to receive one?

It was a dilemma that had been puzzling him for a while and he'd spent a considerable amount of time wondering how to manufacture an opportunity to do so before remembering that he was no longer manufacturing anything when it came to her. But now he thought about it, if the chance to apologise arose this week, then he'd try, because frankly the guilt was driving him insane.

The gravel on the drive crunched, and Leo leapt to his feet and strode over to the window of his first-floor study to see who it was. He watched Abby get out of her car, pause, then turn and bend down to reach for her handbag, and as his entire body tensed and his pulse spiked he told himself once again that he'd made the right decision to reschedule his appointments and come here, because, whatever the secondary benefits, all he was really doing was keeping an eye on what was his.

CHAPTER TWELVE

'SO ARE YOU THERE YET?'

Holding her phone to her ear with one hand and swinging her handbag over her shoulder with the other, Abby smiled because a fortnight on and Gemma sounded as if she was still bristling on her behalf.

'I've literally just arrived,' she said, closing her door and leaning against it for a moment because she could definitely afford to relax enough to have a quick conversation with the best friend who'd been so loyal over the last couple of weeks.

'And is *he* there?'

Seeing as hers was the only car she could spy, apart from a small green hatchback that she presumed belonged to the housekeeper, it didn't look like it. There was certainly no sign of a red—what was it?—V-something-engine, bazillion-horsepower, nought-to-a-hundred-in-a-nanosecond number.

'Nope,' she said, ignoring the faint stab of what she would have suspected was disappointment if being disappointed that he wasn't there weren't completely and utterly absurd.

'I'm very glad to hear it.'

Abby was glad too. Truly she was. She'd half expected her words back there in Leo's car to fall on deaf ears, but to her relief and grim pleasure they hadn't. She'd told him to back off, and that was what he'd done. He'd actually respected her wishes for a change. Exactly as she'd asked.

Those *extremely* rare occasions she'd been tempted to call him up or email him with some totally unnecessary point about the party had been nothing more than blips when she'd temporarily forgotten what he'd done. That was all.

The idea that she might have missed him was risible. She hadn't missed him at all. She hadn't had the chance, and now that she'd finally got round to deleting those damned Google alerts she hadn't been tempted once to see if there was news of him. Not. Once.

'Me too,' she said firmly.

Gemma sniffed. 'He's a scumbag,' she said for what had to be the thousandth time since Abby had told her what had happened.

'Yup.'

He was. And she really *had* to keep remembering it, because lately the tiny part of her that had been flattered at the lengths he'd gone to to win her over when by all accounts he didn't pursue women had been growing, and from time to time she'd found herself wondering whether she hadn't maybe overreacted a bit.

Which was a totally loopy way of thinking, so the sooner this party was over, the better, because she could really do with everything settling back down, her thoughts, her behaviour, her life, basically.

'Is anyone else there?'

'Not yet.' Pulling herself together, Abby glanced at her watch and saw that it was only half past eight. 'But it's still early.'

'What's the place like?'

She looked up and her breath caught. Even though it wasn't the first time she'd seen the house it still made quite an impression. Honey-coloured Cotswold stone against a cloudless blue sky was a happy combination. And then there was the symmetry of the two-storey façade, the balcony that extended above the front door and the rows of large sash windows that appealed to the perfectionist in her.

She wasn't particularly into buildings but she had to admit that everything about this one was easy on the eye. Including its owner.

'It's old. Huge. Lovely,' she said, giving herself a quick kick in the shin, cross for letting herself even think about Leo like that. 'Seventeenth century, maybe. Hundreds of acres. I think the housekeeper said the formal gardens are by Capability Brown. They're beautiful. Then there are woods, fields and a lake out the back. Your average Oxfordshire manor house, basically.'

'What does he do with it all?'

'No idea. But it's in a bit of a state and could do with some serious TLC so he ought to be doing *something*.'

Gemma sighed. 'I wish I could be there.'

'So do I,' said Abby and she meant it—really meant it—because this event was going to be a toughie, although she suspected for none of the usual emergency, safety-pin-needed-type reasons, and she could do with her best friend and colleague.

'Darn celebrity weddings,' said Gemma dryly.

'Especially ones that have been planned for eighteen months.'

'And will probably last six tops.'

Abby grinned. 'Cynic.'

'Realist.'

'Where's that eternal optimism of yours?'

'It's taking a break. Simon didn't call.'

'Oh, no. I'm sorry, sweetie.'

'Par for the course, huh? But never mind. Plenty more fish in the sea, and all that. And talking of fish, isn't lobster on the menu tonight?'

'It certainly is,' said Abby as the mouth-watering menu popped into her head and she switched into work mode.

'It'll be spectacular. Karen's a genius. She won't let you down.'

'I know.'

There was a pause, and then Gemma said, 'Well, look,

I'd better let you get on with it, but if you want to chat, rant or whatever you know where I am.'

'Thanks. Likewise.'

'Hope it goes well.'

'You too.'

'Give the lovely Jake a kiss from me.'

'I will.'

Hanging up with a smile still on her face, Abby pushed herself off her car, and crossed the drive, her trainers crunching on the gleaming white gravel. It was a shame Gemma wasn't going to be around on Saturday, but she'd be fine.

It wasn't as if this were the first time she'd be without her wing woman. It wasn't as if she were going to have time to ruminate over Leo and the way she felt over what he'd done was—a bit worryingly—changing. And it wasn't as if he were here to bring it to the forefront of her mind. Or to distract her or disturb her or just generally upset her equilibrium.

No, she reassured herself, climbing the couple of steps to the front door and ringing the bell. He was probably in London. Or abroad maybe. Anywhere. She didn't know and she genuinely didn't care. As long as he was nowhere to be seen.

The sound of a catch turning snapped her out of her thoughts and she pulled her shoulders back, her smile widening in anticipation of the sight of the friendly and diminutive housekeeper.

But as the door swung open and Abby's gaze fell on legs that were clad in faded blue denim and very definitely male the smile froze on her face because it clearly wasn't Mrs Trimble who'd opened the door.

It was Leo.

And as she looked up and stared at him, for a moment unable to speak although she should have *known* fate might play a trick like this, everything she'd been struggling to convince herself about him over the last fortnight flew straight from her head. All those conversations she'd had with Gemma about how despicably he'd behaved. How badly she'd got him wrong. How dismally disappointing the male sex was in general...

She might as well not have bothered because one look and all she wanted was to throw her arms around his neck, kiss him to bits and tell him how much she'd missed him. Because, as nuts as it sounded given their last encounter, she had. Hugely.

'Leo,' she said with a bright smile even though annoyingly her heart was hammering with something that felt suspiciously like excitement and her stomach was practically liquefying with desire. 'What on earth are you doing here?'

'It's my house.'

'I know, but...' She tailed off helplessly because, really, but what?

But I told you not to show up until the start of the party? But I can't stop thinking about you even though I shouldn't because what you did was so very low? But can't you see that you being here is going to make my job so much harder?

'I want to see how things are done.'

'That's why you have me, though. So you don't have to.'

'I know. But I'm interested. And I might not get another chance. To watch you at work, I mean.' He stopped. Frowned. Ran a hand through his hair and for one heart-stopping second seemed a little unsure of himself, before he gave himself a quick shake and looked at her steadily. 'I also wanted to apologise.'

'For what?'

'You know for what.'

A pang of the hurt that she'd done so well to bury broke free and Abby stifled a sigh. 'Look, Leo, can we please not go there just now?' she said, suddenly a bit weary of it all. 'Whatever's going on, *I'm* at work here and I need to focus.

So I'd really appreciate it if we could leave things at that fo. the next day or two.'

While Leo considered this she could see his jaw tightening, a clear indication that he wasn't happy with her request, but that was tough, because she was here in a professional capacity and, however temporarily, she was calling the shots.

'Fine,' he said eventually. 'But just so as you know, I do want to apologise.'

'If you think you can.'

'I plan to give it a shot. Are you going to come in?'

'Sure,' she said, stepping over the threshold and stiffening as her arm brushed against his chest and what felt like a bolt of electricity shot through her.

'Is my being here really a problem, Abby?'

She stopped in the hallway and turned to find him watching her, his face utterly unreadable.

Of course it was a problem, she thought. It was a huge problem because how on earth was she going to concentrate if he insisted on sticking around, wanting to apologise? But she shook her head and kept her smile pinned to her face. 'Of course it isn't. Not at all. As you pointed out, it's your house. I can hardly order you to leave.'

'Do you *want* me to leave?'

Absolutely she did, but what possible grounds could she have for asking him to do so? It wasn't as if this party were a surprise to *him*. 'I don't mind what you do,' she said with a cool nonchalance that she managed to drum up from who knew where, 'as long as you don't get in the way.'

He gave her the glimmer of a smile. 'I won't.'

But he did.

Not in the way of the streams of people who turned up over the next couple of days, and not, literally speaking, in her way. No, when he wasn't holed up in his study, he took great care not to interfere. He remained very much out of the way, only fully joining in when it came to lunch. Then he'd come over and chat to her about how things were going and ask what was happening next. When lunch was over and everyone got back to work he melted away again. Nevertheless, she knew he was around—somewhere—and that was plenty enough of a distraction.

Vans came and went, disgorging giant urns, a dozen tables and ten times as many chairs, enough linen to sail a tall ship, kitchen equipment, speakers and miles of cabling. Delivery men arrived, dropped off and left. Her subcontractors were everywhere, whirling about, watching the clock and issuing instructions to their teams. Abby herself hovered around, keeping an overall watchful eye on what was going on, clipboard pretty much permanently in hand.

And all the while Leo was there. In her head and in her peripheral vision. Chatting easily to anyone he came across and helping out wherever muscle was needed.

Which was all very well and good but she never knew when or where he was going to pop up next, and as a result she was on edge and slowly going nuts.

However, what could she say without totally giving herself away? What could she do? Absolutely nothing.

Until this morning, that was, when she'd thought she'd had something of a brainwave. Figuring that if she could at least keep him in one place she could be sure to be elsewhere so she wouldn't keep catching sight of him unexpectedly, she'd got him lending a hand to the guys who were putting up the marquee.

But that plan, which had started out successfully enough, had well and truly backfired because an hour or so after she'd given him his orders she'd accidentally seen him and any hope of keeping it together had gone to hell in a handcart, because he'd joined the others in taking off his shirt. And the sight of him pulling on ropes, hammering in pegs, his back bending and flexing, his muscles bunching and twisting, nearly made her pass out with longing.

From then on it had been hard to avoid that area. *So* hard.

Didn't he *know* what the sight of his bare torso did to her? she wondered, heading into the kitchen to see about making tea for whoever wanted it. Surely he had to. So was it deliberate? Perhaps another rotten attempt to get her to yield to his desires and to hell with the apology?

Maybe he did and maybe he was, she thought with a sigh as she filled the tea urn with water and switched it on. She no longer knew which way was up when it came to him, although to be fair it was warm out there and it wasn't as if he were the only one who'd gone shirtless.

Thank goodness there was only a little over twenty-four hours to go till the party. Thank goodness come Sunday morning this horrible confusion hammering away in her head and the awful pressure building inside her would be gone because, frankly, she didn't know how much more of any of it she could take.

Abby had been here for two days already, there was only one left and Leo still hadn't found the opportunity to apologise.

He'd barely even spoken to her. He hadn't had the chance. He'd never much thought about the work that went into an event such as this, yet clearly there was one hell of a lot of it.

While he watched from the sidelines, sometimes from the window of his study where he pretended to be working, sometimes offering to lend a hand, he discovered that Abby, in addition to being gorgeous, sexy and very, very capable, was a dynamo.

She was on the go non-stop from the moment she arrived to the moment she left, her pace dizzying and her energy bottomless, and at the mere thought of the complexity of her job his head swam.

Lunch was the only time she downed tools, and even that

was only for half an hour max. Hardly time for a chat—and he'd tried—let alone an apology. And because she barely paused for breath, he hadn't been able to get her on her own.

But that, he hoped, was about to change.

Impressive though Abby undoubtedly was—and he certainly admired her efficiency, the way she had with people and her frankly extraordinary talent for putting out fires—she was looking exhausted. She arrived at the crack of dawn and left well after dark, and the daily commute to and from London surely couldn't help.

So he'd come up with a plan, this time a truly infallible one.

'Need a hand,' he asked, striding into the kitchen where she was leaning against the work surface and frowning down at the floor as the tea urn beside her hissed away.

Abby jumped, her gaze snapped up and for some reason she went bright red. 'What? Oh? No, thanks. It's just about done.'

'In that case, would you like me to let everyone know tea's ready?'

'Thanks.' Her eyes dipped for a second and then shot back up. 'Is the marquee up?' she asked briskly.

'All done.'

'Then would you mind putting your shirt back on?'

Ah, he thought, smiling inwardly. Not totally unaffected by him, then. 'Does my shirtlessness bother you?'

'Not in the slightest,' she said without batting an eyelid. 'You might catch a chill and I don't think the insurance would cover it. Besides, I have standards to maintain. Order. You know?'

'I do.'

He moved a cup so that out of the fifty or so that sat on the counter the other side of the urn it was the only one with the handle pointing up. She moved it back. And shot him a look.

'I'll put my shirt back on.'

'Thank you.'

'One thing before I round up the troops, though,' he said, deliberately moving towards her.

She took a sidestep away, sliding along the counter, and eyed him warily. 'What?'

'Would you like to stay here tonight?'

Startled, she stared at him, her jaw dropping for a second before she snapped it back up. 'What?'

'Would you like to stay the night?'

She stiffened. Frowned. 'I thought we'd been through this, Leo.'

'I didn't mean with me, although that would be nice.'

'Then what did you mean?'

'You look shattered.'

'Gee, thanks.'

'I'm concerned.'

'There's nothing to be concerned about,' she said with a dismissive wave of her hand. 'It goes with the job. It's fine. It always is.'

'Perhaps I could make it better.'

She arched an eyebrow and said in a voice that could freeze water, 'I'm sure you think you could.'

Leo grinned. 'Not like that.'

'Then how?'

'You get here practically before dawn and you don't leave until at least nine. And I get that you have to, but wouldn't it save time and stress if your commute took five minutes instead of fifty? There are over a dozen spare rooms here. You can take your pick.'

She blinked. 'Oh. Right. Well, that's very thoughtful of you, Leo, but my commute isn't fifty minutes. It's about ten.'

He frowned, faintly taken aback. 'What?'

'I'm staying in a pub in the village.'

Of course she was. Why on earth would she waste time commuting? Hadn't he learnt *anything* about her in the months he'd known her? 'I didn't know.' But he wished he had because then they could have had this conversation two days ago and he wouldn't have worked himself into such knots.

'Why would you?

'Which one?'

'The George.'

'Any good?'

She shrugged. 'It's fine. Not exactly five star but it's clean and has everything I need. The restaurant's pretty terrible, though.'

'OK,' he said slowly as inspiration struck—at the right time, for once. 'Then why don't you come over here for supper?'

Her eyebrows rose. 'Tonight?'

'Yup.'

'With you?'

'I'm afraid so.'

'Oh.'

'We need to talk, Abby.'

'Do we?'

'I'd like to.'

'Hmm.'

If ever there was an advantage to be pressed, this was it, and frankly this was probably his last chance to get her on her own. 'And, you know,' he said casually, putting his hands in the pockets of his jeans and rocking on his heels, 'if you refuse I might start to wonder why the pub's terrible food is more appealing than Mrs Trimble's legendary steak and ale pie. I might start to wonder if it's something to do with me.'

Abby frowned. And after the tiniest of pauses, said, 'Then thank you, Leo. Supper would be great.'

CHAPTER THIRTEEN

At EIGHT O'CLOCK, after a quick shower and a stern talking-to along the lines of making sure she kept her wits about her and her eyes from wandering, Abby was back at Barton Hall, sitting at the huge oak table in the kitchen with a small glass of wine, and watching Leo as he took an incredible-looking pie out of the bottom right oven of the Aga.

As the heavenly scent drifted towards her her mouth watered and her stomach rumbled and she had to admit that it did make a nice change from the rubbery chicken in a basket she'd tried her best to saw through last night.

Not that she'd had much choice about accepting Leo's invitation once he'd issued her with what practically amounted to an ultimatum. It was bad enough that he'd known how strongly the sight of his bare chest affected her. The idea that he might think he had her running scared was simply too much to stomach, so here they were.

'Are you sure I can't do anything to help?' she asked, because she'd been here for a quarter of an hour and so far he hadn't let her lift a finger.

'You could lay the table.'

Glad for something to keep her hands and mind busy, Abby got up and went in search of crockery and cutlery. Five minutes of clattering activity and zero conversation other than a couple of 'knives are in the top drawer' kind of murmurings, the table was laid, and she and Leo were sitting opposite each other with nothing between them except the pie and a bowl of steaming vegetables that sat on a couple of trivets in the centre of the table.

Abby flapped her napkin and laid it on her lap. 'So,' she said brightly because the silence was shifting into decidedly uncomfortable territory and Leo didn't appear to be doing anything to break it. 'You said you wanted to talk, Leo, and here I am.'

Leo had been sitting back, almost lounging in his chair, but now he shifted, straightened a little and tensed. 'Right. Yes.' He stopped, took a deep breath, and then he continued. 'I'm really sorry about the whole *St Jude's* thing, Abby. I can honestly say I don't know what I was thinking.'

She picked up her fork and shot him an arch but not entirely unamused look. 'About your ulterior motive probably. You did have one, didn't you?'

He grimaced. 'Yes.'

'Which was?'

'You know what it was. You even pointed it out.'

'Humour me.' *And humiliate yourself, while you're at it, why don't you? Because you sure humiliated me.*

'Fair enough. I was trying to break down your resistance to me.'

'Why?'

'I don't take rejection well.'

'Who does?'

'I take it exceptionally badly.'

And it didn't take a genius to work out why, she thought, putting a forkful of pie in her mouth and almost groaning with pleasure. Presumably being jilted at the altar in front of all your family and friends could do that to a man.

'So what was it?' she asked. 'Punishment?'

He shook his head, his eyes dark and steady on hers. 'More of an attempt to re-establish the control that I always lose whenever I'm around you.'

Abby reached for her glass of wine, took a sip and thought that *that* was something she could certainly understand. 'The thing is, though,' she said, looking at him thoughtfully, 'I didn't actually reject you. I just put accepting you on hold for a while.'

'I realise that now. But at the time I wasn't thinking all that straight. Patience doesn't seem to be one of my strong points when it comes to you, any more than self-control does.'

As she wasn't sure what to make of that Abby put down her glass and concentrated on eating for a few moments, because honestly the crisp golden pastry was way too irresistible to ignore.

'What you did really didn't show you in your best light, Leo,' she said after a while.

'I know. It's not the way I normally behave.'

'I should hope not.'

'I can't explain it. You seem to bring with you chaos of thought.'

She wasn't quite sure what to make of that either, although she had a certain sympathy for that too. 'I don't mean to. I hate chaos.'

'Nevertheless you do.'

'Is that an excuse?'

'No, because I don't think there *is* an excuse.'

'No.' She put her fork down and looked at him. 'It hurt, you know. I really thought you were being nice. Thoughtful. More fool me.'

For the briefest of moments the impassive mask that was his expression slipped and she caught a flicker of regret. 'I'm sorry. I really don't know what else I can say, although you may be pleased to know that the guilt has been driving me insane.'

A bit rocked by that flash of regret and the admission of guilt, Abby reached for her wine again and toyed with the stem. 'That is some consolation.'

'Do you accept my apology?'

'Is it heartfelt?'

He paused, seemed to tense up a bit, then relaxed and said, 'Very much so.'

And because of the way he said it, she found herself softening. 'Then in that case, yes.'

'Thank you,' he said, giving her a faint smile that had her heart lurching and her mouth going oddly dry.

Leo carried on looking at her and Abby found she couldn't break the contact. The seconds ticked by, the air thickening and the tension between them creeping back and she could feel her heart rate quickening, the roar of her blood in her ears.

Conversation. That was what they needed now. Nice, normal conversation. About the party. That would be good. That would be safe.

'So, forty years,' she said brightly and he jumped, as if he'd been lost in thought and she'd yanked him out of it. 'Quite an achievement.'

'Hmm,' said Leo, picking up his fork and finally tucking in to both the food and the chat. 'How long have your parents been married?'

'Thirty-five. Kind of incredible, don't you think?'

'Remarkable. Have you never been tempted?'

'I've never been asked.'

His eyebrows shot up. 'I find that surprising.'

'Why?'

'Because you're beautiful, successful, warm, intelligent and kind, for a start.'

'Oh,' she said faintly, reeling a bit at her apparent attributes. 'Thank you.'

'You're welcome.'

'Though you missed out "forgiving".'

'Thoughtless of me.'

'Only I have been told I'm not very dateable.'

'Not very dateable?' he said, glancing up and looking at her as if she'd suddenly sprouted another head, which, she had to admit, did send her self-esteem shooting through the roof.

'According to my last boyfriend, I'm too independent and too capable,' she said, her self-esteem plummeting again as the memory of Martin detailing all her faults shot into her head.

Leo frowned. 'And that's bad?'

'Apparently it's intimidating.'

'Only to someone with an inferiority complex.'

'Not something you suffer from,' she said with a smile.

He arched an eyebrow. 'You'd be surprised.'

Whatever that might mean Abby couldn't be sure. And besides, her mind was now on something else entirely because for the first time it was occurring to her that maybe she wasn't only too capable and too independent, but also perhaps a bit too demanding. Maybe because she expected so much from herself, she expected too much from the men she went out with.

Or maybe not. Whatever. There wasn't time now to indulge in a bout of self-analysis. She'd have to save that for later.

'Well, with hindsight,' she said, hauling herself back to the conversation, 'he was completely crappy and I can't believe I wasted four months of my life on him.' Which was all true, whether she'd expected too much of him or not.

'If it's any comfort, I wanted to date you.'

While Leo picked up his glass and drained what was left of the contents, Abby dropped her fork and it clattered onto the plate, her head wiped clean of everything but what he'd just said. 'You did?' she said faintly. 'When?'

'The day after we slept together. I called you.'

'That's right. To discuss the party.'

Leo shook his head. 'Not to discuss the party. I was going to ask you out.'

'Why didn't you?'

'Because you told me you weren't interested before I could.'

'I did.' She frowned as she struggled to work out what that meant. 'So the whole party thing was…what?'

He shrugged. Looked away for a second. 'An attempt to save face, I suppose.'

'Oh,' she murmured, confused because on the one hand the knowledge that he'd wanted to take her out was pretty confidence boosting, but on the other she'd spent the last couple of months working hard on something that she'd thought was a labour of love but in actual fact had been a mere whim, which wasn't confidence boosting in the slightest. 'That sounds a bit desperate.'

'You have no idea.' He went to fill their glasses, pouring wine into only his when she covered hers and said that she was driving.

'Do you regret it?'

'Not for one moment,' he said with such conviction that she couldn't help believe him.

'I'm glad.' And not just about that because it was weirdly comforting to know that he'd been making as many rash decisions as she had. 'It's going to be a great party.'

'It is.' He paused, then said casually, 'So just out of interest, if I had asked you out, what would you have said?'

Given how honest Leo was being, Abby didn't see any reason to be otherwise. 'No.'

His eyebrows shot up. 'Seriously?'

She grinned. 'Is it that hard to believe?'

'Honestly? After a night like the one we had, it is a bit, yes.'

'I've been attracted to you since the moment I laid eyes on you, Leo. You know I have. And I still am. You know that too. But the thing is, unfortunately you're just not my type.'

'Why not?'

'Emotions.'

At the word, he winced, and Abby arched an eyebrow. 'My point exactly.'

'Which is what?'

'You don't like emotions, do you?'

'What makes you say that?'

'Well, the wince for one thing is a bit of a giveaway.'

Leo shrugged. 'OK, so I'm not a great fan of emotion. Most men aren't. It's not a crime.'

'No. But I am.'

'So I've come to realise,' he said dryly. 'And the problem is…?'

'The problem is, in my experience, that bottling things up, not saying what you think, what you want, what you feel, can be seriously bad for your health, and I don't want to be with someone like that.'

Leo's eyes glittered in the dim light of the kitchen. 'Seems to work OK for me.'

'It didn't work so well for my father.'

There was a pause, and then, 'The heart attack?'

'Exactly.'

Leo frowned. 'You said it wasn't fatal.'

'It wasn't. But while he's sort of fine, he's never fully recovered.'

'I'm sorry to hear that, but heart attacks do happen.'

'But in this case it needn't have,' said Abby shortly, and had to remind herself to remain calm. 'He'd lost his job, and because of his pride, because of his inability to communicate properly, he couldn't tell my mother. According to the doctors the chances are that it wouldn't have happened if he'd shared the burdens he carried. But he wouldn't. And the really annoying, really ridiculous thing is, he's still doing it. He's so emotionally repressed it makes me want to tear my hair out. Especially when my brothers, who've inherited his stiff-upper-lip thing, start doing exactly the same.'

'I see,' said Leo, with a tilt of his head. 'And you think I'm emotionally repressed too?'

'I do, Leo. I do.' Abby looked back at him and, as his mouth curved into the faintest—slightly mocking?—smile, lost all sense of calm and asked hotly, 'Don't you ever, I don't know, want to throw things?'

He stared at her, bemused. 'Such as what?'

'Anything. It doesn't matter.'

'Why would I want to throw things?'

'To release the build-up of emotion.'

'I never need to. I never have a build-up of emotion.'

'That's exactly my point. You should. Otherwise how do you know you're feeling?'

'I don't. And honestly, I don't see that as a negative.'

'I'm sure you don't.'

'So what other evidence do you have for your theory that I'm emotionally repressed? Surely it can't only be my lack of throwing things.'

Oh, where to start…?

Well, as he was treating what mattered deeply to her with nothing more than mild amusement and it was beginning to seriously piss her off, how about the jugular? 'Why don't you tell me about your marriage, Leo?' she said, fixing her gaze to his and resolving not to let go whatever happened.

There was a second of absolute silence before his eyes narrowed a fraction and he answered. 'What on earth are you talking about?' he said, his tone a good degree or two chillier than a moment ago. 'I'm not married.'

'I know. But you nearly were once.'

And now his jaw was tightening, almost imperceptibly, but she was beginning to recognise the tiny signs that on the odd occasion gave him away. 'How do you know about that?'

'Something on the internet.'

'Where?'

'I'll send you the link.'

'Thanks.'

'I guess you'll be wanting to hush that up too.'

He frowned. 'What?'

'How did you keep what happened so quiet? How did you keep it out of the papers?'

'I have loyal family and friends. So does Lisa. How much do you know?'

'I know she left you at the altar for some guy she'd got back in touch with on Facebook.'

'She married him. They have a child.'

'And how do you feel about it all?'

'I don't feel anything.'

Abby's eyebrows shot up. 'Seriously?'

'Why would I? It happened five years ago.'

'And at the time?'

This time there was nothing imperceptible about the way his jaw clenched and his face darkened. 'I handled it,' he said and it occurred to her that, however he'd handled it, it hadn't been well.

'So how come you still have a problem with the time of year and you haven't slept with anyone since her? Other than me, I mean,' she added, and her cheeks heated.

Leo's gaze snapped to hers. 'What on earth are you talking about?'

'Jake said you hadn't had a woman in your bed for years.'

'Doesn't mean I haven't been in their beds,' said Leo dryly. 'You weren't the first by any means.'

And you won't be the last, so don't think you're anything special was the very clear message, and for a moment it knocked her a bit sideways.

'Oh. No. Well. Of course not,' she said, swiftly rallying because she didn't want to be special to a man who held such an opposing view to something she valued so highly. 'Jake's obviously got the wrong end of the stick.'

'I don't see the need to discuss my sex life with him. And

I really don't have a problem with the time of year any more. It would be absurd to be hung up on something that happened so long ago. I genuinely couldn't care less about it.'

Which well and truly told her. 'And the shutting off of your emotions?'

'Habit.'

'Oh, but it's such a bad one.'

'You're the expert.'

'I am, which is how I know that the more you suppress emotion, the harder it becomes to control and the more you end up dwelling on it.'

'Just as well I don't have any, then.'

'And if that isn't a good reason to let it all out,' she said, ignoring him because he might like to think that but everyone had *some* and he was fooling himself if he thought he was different, 'then I don't know what is.'

'How do you let it all out?'

'I don't have to, because I never let it become a problem. Whatever I'm feeling I embrace it. If I'm happy I say so. If I'm not, I say it too.'

A spark of something—challenge? Smugness? Glee?—lit the depths of Leo's eyes and, despite the heat that the Aga was churning out, Abby shivered.

'What are you feeling now?' he asked lazily, which had her guard up because laziness wasn't a tone she'd ever heard him employ before.

'Full. Tired. Excited about tomorrow.'

'That's it?'

'More or less.'

'You're a hypocrite, Abby.'

She blinked. 'I'm a what?'

'A hypocrite.'

'No, I'm not.'

'Yes, you are. For all your talk about saying what you feel, what you want, you won't admit you still want me.'

At the gleam in his eye Abby's heart lurched and her breath caught in her throat. OK, now they were heading into seriously dangerous territory because in the blink of an eye she'd lost control of the conversation. Leo was now in the driving seat and would take her along a route that would end up with her all tangled up because she didn't know *what* she wanted. The thought-chaos thing went both ways.

Making a great show of looking at her watch and yawning, Abby shot him a bright smile. 'Well, it's a big day tomorrow,' she said, pushing her chair back and wondering whether her legs would be steady enough to support her long enough for her to get to her car. 'So I think I should go.'

'Of course you do,' he said dryly. 'But before you run off, let me put my cards on the table once and for all. I'm not looking for a relationship, Abby. I haven't had one since Lisa. And that suits me fine because absolutely *nothing* will persuade me to go there again. But I want you. And I want an affair with you. Short and hot and satisfying until it ends. That's all. Emotion, or lack of it, needn't come into it. Think about it.'

All through the journey back to the pub, the usual quick chat with Sheila, the barmaid, and her preparations for bed Abby thought about little else.

An affair.

Out of the question, she'd thought, parking her car and getting out.

Tempting, she'd thought, wishing Sheila goodnight and heading up the stairs.

Out of the question, she'd thought, squeezing toothpaste onto the toothbrush and brushing her teeth with vigour.

Hmm.

It was frustrating, this inability to work out what she wanted. More than that, actually. It was infuriating. She'd thought she had it sussed. That nothing would ever come of the chemistry they shared. But now that Leo had tossed out the suggestion of an affair, she was no longer sure.

He'd told her exactly what he wanted from her, but what did she want from him?

Now, there was a question.

She wanted sex, that much was true. And she wanted it badly. She might as well admit it.

But what else?

Well, nothing, because he didn't have anything else to offer, and she wasn't ever again going to make the mistake of thinking he'd change on that front.

And was that really such a bad thing?

Flinging back the covers and getting into bed, Abby gave in and decided that maybe it wasn't. By his own admission he wasn't up for a relationship, and actually neither was she, at least not with him. Oh, she wouldn't mind a boyfriend at some point in the future, but that clearly wasn't going to be Leo.

In the meantime, though, and in the absence of a man who would be perfect boyfriend material, why shouldn't she go for some hot, no-strings sex? Why shouldn't she have some fun? She'd been working incredibly hard recently. Didn't she deserve it?

Therefore what would be so wrong with an affair with him?

In fact, might it not instead be a teeny bit fabulous?

CHAPTER FOURTEEN

THE DAY OF the party dawned bright and clear. And, for Abby, early. Not that she minded. She always woke up pumping with adrenalin and raring to go the day of an event, and this one had an extra edge, because tonight, when it was all over, she was going to take Leo to bed.

Oh, yes, she was, because it wasn't only the day that had dawned bright and clear. Abby had too, and she now knew exactly what she wanted. Leo. For as short or as long as it lasted. Therefore she was going to get him into bed, and, seeing as how she didn't anticipate much resistance, once she'd got him in it she wasn't going to let him out, for the rest of the weekend at least.

The thought of it, the excitement and the anticipation, kept her going through the long day of final preparations. It gave everything she did an urgency she'd never experienced before, because unlike every other event she'd organised she was wishing away the hours, wishing away the party.

But the hours did pass, and in contrast to how churned up she felt inside they passed remarkably smoothly, as proven by her emergency kit being down by only one roll of duct tape, an extension cord and four sticking plasters.

Apart from a last-minute change to the table plan to accommodate the now non-attendance of Jake's former date—which, with all the after-party plans swimming around in her head, she didn't even lament much—nothing major had gone wrong.

Tables were now laid and flowers were arranged. The caterers were on schedule and the string quartet was tuning up.

Parking attendants had been given their instructions and the waiting staff had been briefed. Everything was poised on a knife edge. Everyone was ready for the off.

Of Leo she'd seen neither hide nor hair all day, and for that she was grateful because if she had seen him she might well not have been able to wait till tonight to make her fantasies reality. But now, since all that remained to do was let him know how he was going to spend the night, she had to seek him out.

Having left her car in the field and road-tested the walkway designed to protect shoes from mud, Abby found him in the marquee.

He was standing in a corner of the tent, his gaze slowly sweeping over the tables, the decorations, and the giant arrangements of white hydrangeas that sat in urns planted about the place and the balloons tied to each chair, just sort of looking and faintly smiling. She stood in another corner and did the same, although her gaze was sweeping over him and not the room she now knew every inch of.

He wore black tie very well, she thought, her heart slowly flipping while heat and longing began to spread through her. He was so gorgeous. So intriguing. So complicated. And so perfect for a fling.

Propelled by the thought of that, she walked over to him. Halfway there, he noticed her. Turned and ran his eyes slowly down the length of her and back up, and by the time he'd finished and she was right in front of him her mouth was dry and her pulse was racing.

'So, this is the calm before the storm,' he murmured, his eyes dark, his expression inscrutable.

She nodded, and swallowed hard. 'Ten minutes or so to go.'

'It looks incredible.'

'It does.'

'So do you.'

'Thank you.'

'You're welcome.'

'Are you looking forward to it?'

Leo gave her the glimmer of a smile. 'Contrary to all my expectations, I think I am a bit.'

Despite the heat, Abby couldn't help inwardly flinching. 'Were your expectations really that bad?'

'Not at all. Seriously, Abby. I never doubted you for a moment. I just don't really like giving parties.'

'Oh,' she said, mollified by the first half of what he said, taken aback by the second. 'Why not?'

'Being centre of attention doesn't really appeal.'

Leo's smile faded and Abby figured that given what had happened the afternoon of his wedding it was hardly surprising. 'At this one you won't be centre of attention. Or, at least, you shouldn't be.'

'True.'

Silence fell and it wasn't comfortable at all, so, taking a deep breath, she summoned up her courage and looked him straight in the eye because she had to say this. Now. Before either someone came or she chickened out. 'You were right, last night, Leo.'

He went still. Tilted his head and looked at her, his eyes guarded. 'In what way?'

'I have been a hypocrite. Sort of. I haven't told you what I want, although, in my defence, last night I didn't really know.'

A tiny muscle hammered in his jaw. 'But now you do?'

'Very much so.'

'And?'

She leaned in close. Breathed him in and might have swayed towards him slightly before catching the sound of distant voices and easing back. 'Carriages are at midnight,' she said, wishing for a moment that she and Leo were anywhere but here. 'Meet me at the folly at one and I'll tell you everything then.'

His dark eyes glittered. 'I'll be there.'

How the hell he was supposed to concentrate on the party after that Leo had no idea. He was dimly aware of the guests arriving, of various family members and friends shaking him by the hand or clapping him on the back. He was vaguely aware of the buzz of chatter, the hum of stealthy excitement as everyone gathered in the marquee.

But all he could really think about was that there were six hours between now and the time he'd be meeting Abby. Three hundred and sixty minutes. Twenty-one thousand six hundred seconds, and every one of them was going to take a decade to tick by. He just knew it.

They didn't, of course. In fact, once Jake arrived with his parents time flew. He didn't think he'd ever forget the looks on their faces when they walked into the marquee. The utter astonishment, the shock, and then a minute or two later the beaming delight. He didn't think he'd forget the warm glow it gave him inside in a hurry either.

Champagne flowed, canapés were consumed, and for the first time in he couldn't remember how long Leo didn't want to stand at the edge and merely observe the proceedings with one eye on the clock. He wasn't searching for excuses to leave conversations. Instead he was actually seeking conversation out. Laughing and joking with Jake. Mingling and being a host, and a congenial one at that, because while he'd told Abby that he was looking forward to the party, he hadn't really expected to enjoy himself. But he was. A lot.

So when it came to sitting down for dinner, Leo was still chuckling about a story a barrister friend of his father's had just told him regarding the extraordinary defence an alleged embezzler had mounted, and didn't notice his mother looking at him curiously.

'This is a lovely party, darling,' she said, once they'd sat down and he'd poured her some wine. 'Thank you.'

'Not really sure it's me you should be thanking, Mum.'

'Why not? It was your idea, wasn't it?'

Leo shifted on his chair, remembering how the party had come about and feeling slightly uncomfortable. 'But not my execution.'

He turned to fill up the glass of his cousin, who was sitting on his other side, and momentarily went still, warm, and oddly dry-mouthed when he caught sight of Abby standing at the entrance to the marquee, clipboard, as ever, in hand.

'She's quite a girl,' said his mother.

'She certainly is,' he muttered, dragging his gaze away and concentrating on putting the bottle down since his hand seemed to be shaking a little.

'It's good to see you smiling,' she said and he wondered why that would come on the back of a comment about Abby. Although now he thought about it, his mother hadn't actually mentioned Abby by name, had she? Which meant that, damn, he'd given her an opportunity to read far too much into something that was nothing.

Nevertheless he'd better stop looking out for her if he didn't want his mother jumping to the wholly wrong conclusion. There'd be plenty of time to look later in any case. With any luck.

'Am I?' he said as coolly as he could.

'You are. Properly. For the first time in years.'

And was it really any surprise? Of course he was smiling. Tonight Abby was going to be his. He was sure of it. Why else would she have given him a look that could have melted ice when she'd told him to meet her at the folly?

'Yes, well, I'm happy,' he said, and he was, because the thought of what the night hopefully held in store was truly delightful.

Not that his mother needed to know the details.

Half expecting her to probe further, when she didn't Leo glanced at her, saw that her eyes were shining a bit too brightly, and he wordlessly handed her his handkerchief, just about resisting the urge to roll his eyes.

However, the tears, unfortunately, didn't stop there. Jake's speech, which began by thanking Elsa Brightman—radiant and beaming in green—Abby—gorgeous, wonderful, and he hoped very shortly to occupy his bed—and everyone who'd worked so hard to make tonight a success, became suitably sentimental.

His brother, who'd never had his kind of trouble with emotion, had virtually everyone reaching for their tissues. There were sounds of noses being blown across the marquee. His mother spent the entire five minutes the speech lasted alternately sobbing and laughing. He'd caught his father surreptitiously dabbing his eyes with his napkin. At one point, to his absolute horror he'd even felt a quick tightening of his own throat.

But that had passed swiftly enough, as had the video, which had had part of him wallowing in nostalgia, part of him cringing with embarrassment.

And after a sublime, appropriately red-inspired supper of silky smooth gazpacho, lobster thermidor and raspberry and champagne jelly he was even persuaded to hit the dance floor. To a string of seventies hits he danced with his mother, his aunts and, after much cajoling, his ninety-eight-year-old grandmother.

But not Abby. Leo didn't trust himself to dance with her, even if she had been around to ask. As she'd pointed out, he wasn't centre of attention tonight, and as the clock ticked he increasingly became wound so tightly he knew that if he held her in his arms he—they—might well become the star attraction.

By the time the guests started wandering outside to let off balloons and watch the fireworks, gently corralled by an ever-efficient party planner, Leo could hardly stand the tension inside him.

He watched her out of the corner of his eye, felt desire punch him in the stomach and something else wallop him in the chest—anticipation most likely—and thought, Not long to go now.

Standing to one side of the group of guests, just outside the marquee, Abby dropped her head back and watched one hundred and twenty red heart-shaped balloons drift off into the moonlit night.

She was still there smiling gently and her thoughts similarly drifting when five minutes later the sky lit up with rockets, star bursts and a heart-shaped Catherine wheel before climaxing in a wonderful finale consisting of a giant four zero that crackled and fizzled and bathed everything in soft golden fire.

Forty years, she thought wistfully. Forty years. What would it be like to spend that long with one other person? To live with them, love them, argue and make up with them...

It was a lifetime, and she simply couldn't imagine it. Or maybe she could. With someone like Leo, only not so emotionally closed off. Someone strong, loving, supportive and loyal. Someone who'd tease her, cherish her and not be afraid to let go in front of her.

Definitely not Leo, then.

Although, come to think of it, he hadn't seemed all that emotionally distant tonight, had he? She might have been flat-out busy, but that hadn't stopped her noticing him chatting to the guests, smiling, even laughing a little. She'd seen how he'd responded to Jake's speech, and the film—which when she'd first seen it had made her all soft and gooey inside—and how he'd tried to hide it. And she'd seen how he'd danced with most of his female relatives and, as she hadn't caught even the hint of a grimace, he'd clearly enjoyed it.

So maybe there was hope for him yet.

She hoped there was. She really hoped there was. Because if that were the case then maybe they had a chance. Of something more than a fling. Of a relationship, perhaps. Maybe even one that lasted forty years...

She smiled dreamily at the thought of that for a lovely moment or two, and then the truth behind it hit her and her smile vanished. As if she'd been punched in the stomach, she gasped for breath. Reeled. And then wobbled, her knees shaking and feeling as if they were about to give way and she suddenly went icy cold.

Oh, no.

Oh, no, oh, no, oh, *no*.

She didn't just want someone *like* Leo. She wanted *him*. For ever, because—oh, crap—she was in love with him. Head over heels in love with him. With every inch of him, with everything he was and everything he wasn't.

Why else had she forgiven him so quickly for the diabolical way he'd behaved over the *St Jude's* visit? Hadn't she even thought she was utterly mad for still wanting him after what he'd done? She had because even back then she'd loved him.

How the hell had it happened? she wondered frantically as everyone around her oohed and aahed with delight and her world collapsed. When? And why? She couldn't work it out. She couldn't work anything out. Her head was a jumbled mess, a fuzzy, blurry, tangled mess.

The only thing she did know, as certainly as she knew her own name, was that she was completely and irreversibly in love with him, and she was therefore doomed.

Because Leo wasn't in love with her. And he wouldn't ever be. So she'd thought he might have been softening this evening, might have been allowing a little emotion into his life.

But that didn't mean anything for her, did it? Of course it didn't. She wasn't making that mistake again. And how could she possibly forget the conviction with which he'd told her last night that *absolutely nothing* would persuade him to change his stance on relationships? She couldn't.

But nor now could she possibly embark on a fling with him. It would destroy her, knowing that she was in it hoping for for ever and he was only in it for as long as she held his interest. She just couldn't do it.

As her watch beeped midnight Abby jumped, came to and saw that all around her guests were milling, saying their goodbyes and their thank yous, which meant that she had to meet Leo in an hour, and the conversation she'd planned, the *things* she'd planned, were history because everything had now irrevocably changed.

Hexagonal in shape and having seen its fair share of romantic trysts, the folly was by the lake and, tonight, lit by the full moon. The arches were in shadow and the patches of stone that the moss hadn't yet reached gleamed pale in the silvery light. The only sounds were the faint breeze that blew in off the lake, the rustling from nearby trees and the thud of his footsteps along the path.

Not that Leo gave a damn about the atmosphere.

All he cared about as he strode towards the folly at a couple of minutes before the appointed hour was the woman he hoped to meet within. Meet, haul into his arms and carry off to his bed, with any luck.

And there she was. Standing beneath one of the arches, her face pale in the moonlight but so lovely that his heart turned over and he nearly missed his footing.

'Hi,' he said when he reached her, vaguely wondering whether it would be a bit presumptuous to take her in his arms and kiss her senseless before he'd heard what she had to say.

'Hi,' she said, although her smile seemed strained.

'Well?'

Abby took a deep breath and the tension inside him wound tighter than he'd have thought possible.

'I nearly didn't come.'

Leo went still, some sixth sense alerting him to the fact that something wasn't quite right. What the hell? Hadn't they got beyond games? 'Why not?'

'Because I thought I could do this, then I realised I couldn't. But I have to because I may be many things but I'm not a hypocrite.'

'I don't understand,' he said with a frown.

'How do you feel about me, Leo?'

Huh? What? What was this? Hadn't he already told her? Well, that was fine. If she needed reassurance he'd give it to her. 'I want you. A lot. More than I've ever wanted anyone before.'

'Is that it?'

No, of course that wasn't it. 'I like you. Enormously. I admire you and respect you. I think you're great.'

She shook her head, her face sad. 'It's not enough.'

'How can it not be enough?' he asked, running his hands through his hair for something to do with them because he was now genuinely perplexed and not a little alarmed.

'It just isn't.'

'Why not?'

'Because the thing is, Leo, you don't want a relationship, and I, I've discovered, do. Specifically, with you. A long one. Maybe even the for-ever kind.'

'What?' he said faintly, not getting—maybe not wanting to get—what she was talking about.

'I'm in love with you, Leo. Totally in love with you. You bring disorder to my order and try as I might I don't dislike it. You hurt me, and I let it go. You're the man I can imagine spending the rest of my life with, the only man. So I really, *really* wish I could have a fling with you but I can't. It would just be too awful when it finished.'

If someone had hit him over the head with a branch Leo couldn't have been more stunned. He couldn't think. Couldn't speak. Could barely remain upright, because, damn, this was not the way he'd expected their rendezvous to go.

'And I know that's not what you wanted to hear,' she continued, very calm, very controlled, 'so I don't expect you to do or say anything in response. You've made your position on the subject of relationships very clear, and that's fair enough. I understand it. But nevertheless I can't help the way I feel. So I'm sorry, Leo, I really am, but I think it's best if we say goodbye.'

And with that, she walked over to him, gave him a brief, searing kiss on the mouth that blitzed his brain and rooted him to the spot, and, after a couple of moments during which she looked at him as if trying to peer into his soul, was gone.

Don't look back, don't look back, don't look back.

And though it cost her what remained of her shattered self-control Abby didn't. She left Leo standing there in the folly after the toughest speech she'd ever had to make, and with every step she took away from him her vision blurred a little bit more and her heart broke into ever tinier pieces.

But she didn't look back. She couldn't. If she had, she'd have run back to him just as fast as she could, told him she'd made a horrendous mistake and embarked on the fling right then and there.

How she'd got through those awful five or so minutes without falling to her knees and begging him to reconsider his position on relationships she'd never know. But she'd done the right thing. She had. For once. Because she couldn't change him, and he clearly had no intention of doing so himself. She'd come to believe she was right. Eventually. When she stopped hurting so badly.

Once clear of the folly she picked up speed and ran through the garden, narrowly avoiding Jake and the look of astonishment on his face as she streaked past, skirted round the marquee, along the walkway.

And it was only when she made it to the safety of her car, by this time all on its own in the field, that the adrenalin that had kept her going drained away, leaving her with nothing to do other than slump over the steering wheel and burst into tears.

CHAPTER FIFTEEN

'Are you all right, Leo?'

At the sound of his brother's voice somewhere above and in front of him, Leo froze for a second but he didn't stop. 'No, I'm not bloody all right,' he said, gritting his teeth as he heaved on the skiff and with a groan and a creak it moved another foot down the ramp.

'What on earth are you doing?'

'What does it look like?'

'It looks like you're planning to take a boat out onto the lake,' said Jake dryly, 'but you can't be doing that because if you were you'd have completely and utterly lost—your—mind.'

'Then I've lost my mind.'

'It's half past one in the morning.'

'I am aware of that.'

'And you suddenly have the urge to go for a row?'

'I need to think.'

'Can't you do that in the house?'

'No, I can't.'

'Why, what's up?'

Pretty much at the end of his tether with himself, Abby, everything, Leo shot up and glared at his brother. 'Are you just going stand there asking pointless questions or are you going to help me?'

'I'll do better than help you,' said Jake easily, clearly not fazed in the slightest by his lousy temper. 'I'll join you.'

'That won't be necessary.'

'Well, that's tough, because you're obviously in a state,

and I'm not letting you go out on that—' he pointed to the lake '—in that—' he pointed to the boat '—alone.'

Leo shrugged and braced himself for another heave. He didn't have either the time or the inclination to argue. There was quite enough going on in his head as it was. 'Fine,' he muttered. 'Whatever. Just help me get this sodding thing into the water.'

Jake strode forward, leaned down and pushed as Leo pulled and two minutes later the boat was afloat and carrying two black-tied passengers, one dark and scowling and pulling on the oars as if his life depended on it, the other just as dark, but concerned and wary as he leaned forwards, his elbows on his knees.

'So are you going to tell me what this is all about?' said Jake as they glided through the water towards the centre of the dark gloomy lake.

'Nope.'

'Oka-a-ay-y-y, then. I'll consider myself just along for the ride.'

'As long as you don't speak,' said Leo, gritting his teeth and feeling his muscles burn, 'I don't care what you do.'

Jake leaned back and made a point of inhaling deeply and looking around him interestedly, as if it were midday instead of midnight, but seemed to have taken the hint, thank goodness, because at long last he'd shut up.

And so now he, Leo, could finally *think*. Finally try and work out what had happened back there in the folly. And what he made of it all.

Abby had said she didn't expect him to say or do anything, but how could he have? She hadn't given him a chance. Not that he'd have known what to say even if she had. He'd been poleaxed by her revelation. Unable to think, let alone speak.

But now, with the tension seeping from his body, he could. In a minute. When his head cleared. Not that it seemed to be doing so.

As his muscles burned Leo gritted his teeth. Maybe going through it all out loud instead might make it easier to understand. Maybe his brother might provide the insight he so badly lacked. At least the darkness would provide some sort of protection. He didn't know if he'd be contemplating this in broad daylight. He was going to feel pretty stripped as it was. But he had to try *something* because he was driving himself mad.

After one last pull, he leaned down on the oars, and levered them up out of the water, leaving the boat at the whim of the breeze.

'The problem is Abby,' he said eventually, the words sounding oddly loud in the silence of the night.

'I wondered if it might be.'

'Things have been…I don't know exactly…but, well, developing, I suppose. Not without hiccups, but maybe going somewhere. Slowly.'

'No kidding,' said Jake, his wide grin very visible in the moonlight and very annoying.

Leo scowled. 'It's not remotely amusing.'

Jake's grin faded. Sort of. 'No. Sorry.'

'So half an hour ago I met her in the folly. I thought she was going to tell me she was up for a fling but instead she told me she loved me.'

There was a moment's silence, and then came Jake's soft, 'Ah.'

Leo frowned. 'Why did she *do* that?'

Jake shrugged and lifted his hands palm up in the 'beats the hell out of me' kind of way. 'Who knows? But she's a woman and shifting the goalposts just when you think you know where they are, asking for more when you think what you're giving them is plenty, does tend to be a speciality of theirs.'

'Tonight I really thought we were on the same wavelength,' said Leo, shaking his head in bafflement, 'but you know, I don't think we've ever been on the same wavelength.'

'Doesn't sound like it. But then what man ever is?'

'She's big into emotion.'

'And you're not.'

'No,' he said, waiting for the customary shudder, which oddly enough didn't come. Although maybe it wasn't that odd because hadn't he sort of opened up a bit this evening? And hadn't it been, well, not too bad? Hadn't he had a glimpse of how much richer his life could be if he let himself feel, truly feel, and kind of liked it?

'So, at the risk of sounding all touchy-feely,' said Jake, thankfully cutting into his thoughts because, given that they represented a one-eighty-degree change to the way he'd lived perfectly happily for the last five years, they were faintly disturbing ones, 'she's told you how she feels about you, but how do you feel about her?'

'I don't know.'

'All right, then. How do you feel in general?'

'Right now?'

Jake nodded.

'Pissed off. Confused. Like I don't know which way is up any more.'

'It all seems pretty clear to me.'

'Does it? Really? Because I don't know what the hell's going on.'

'Come on, Leo,' said Jake, a little impatiently. 'Use your brain and work it out.'

'I can't.'

Jake let out a deep sigh of what sounded like exasperation. 'Fine,' he said. 'If you insist on sticking your stubborn head in the sand, then let me break it down for you in easy-to-answer questions. Only don't think about the answers too much. Deal?'

Well, what option did he have? He wanted to know what

was going on so that he could do something about it, but he just couldn't seem to see the wood for the trees. 'Deal.'

'OK, then. Here we go. Do you like her?'

Leo nodded. 'A lot.'

'What do you like about her?'

'Everything.'

'How would you feel if you never saw her again?'

'Lost.'

'What else?'

'Desolate. Wretched. Pointless.'

'How would you feel if I told you she was standing on the ramp, watching us?'

His heart pounded at about two hundred beats per minute and his head swam. 'Ecstatic. Relieved. Nervous.' He took in a slow breath, then said, 'Is she?'

'No. So now how do you feel?'

He didn't have to think about it. 'Crushed.'

'Do you love her?'

'Yes.'

'At long last,' said Jake with a grin. 'Thank God for that. My work here is done.'

But Leo wasn't listening any longer. He was too busy reeling all over again because how could he have been so thick? How could he have been so blind? It was *so* obvious.

He was in love with her. Of course he was. Deeply and madly. She'd turned his life upside down. Had him behaving totally out of character and doing things that logic and reason utterly defied, and, while it had been baffling him for weeks, now it all made sense.

He'd spent so long trying to avoid love he hadn't recognised it. It had hit him with the force of a sledgehammer and like a fool he'd mistaken it for mere lust. But it wasn't just lust and he didn't want her for just a fling. He wanted her for ever.

'I'm nuts about her,' he said faintly.

'Seems that way.'

As the knowledge took root and spread Leo could feel his entire body fill with emotion. Everything he'd tried to keep at bay for these last few months, last few years, in all likelihood. His heart was thundering with it; his head was churning with it. He felt dizzy, overwhelmed, about to explode.

'I think I need to throw something,' he said, finally understanding what Abby had meant about releasing the build-up of pressure.

'What?'

'Only there's nothing here to throw.'

He glanced at his brother and Jake's eyebrows shot up in horror. 'Don't look at me.'

'I've been an idiot.'

And now that the scales had fallen from his eyes and his deepest fears were bubbling to the surface he knew perfectly well why. The hurt, the failure, the fear.

And therein lay the problem, he thought, his heart plummeting for a moment as all those feelings of pain and inadequacy rushed back, because he might be in love with Abby but that didn't mean that everything was suddenly wonderful. That didn't mean that history wouldn't repeat itself.

But nor did it mean that it would.

So did he dare hope that this time things would be different? Was she *it*? And was he prepared to take the risk to find out?

He was, because she was incredible, he adored her, and the idea of not taking the risk, of letting her go, of not having her in his life was simply unbearable so he really had no option.

'I need to go and find her,' he said, his pulse galloping with the desire to see if he could sort out the mess they were in.

'It's late. The pub will be closed.'

'There's a lock-in. I overheard one of the waitresses mentioning it.'

Jake grinned. 'Then what are you waiting for?'

'And you know the worst thing?' said Abby glumly, sitting at the bar and staring down into her second shot of tequila. 'I have the feeling it's partly my fault.'

'How can it be?' said Sheila, who stood behind the bar with her hand on the bottle and a clear intention to keep the tequila coming. 'You told him you loved him, and he just stood there. Silently.' She sniffed dismissively. 'Pillock.'

What with a lousy ex-husband who refused to pay the child support he owed, Sheila, Abby had discovered over the last couple of days, didn't have all that great an opinion of men.

Yet despite what had happened back there in that folly, Abby *did*, especially of Leo, and the problem she had now was that he wasn't a pillock. He really wasn't. He was the man of her dreams and unavailable, and in the twenty minutes it had taken her to pull herself together and drive back to the pub, during which her mind hadn't stopped, she'd come to the miserable, heartbreaking conclusion that she'd utterly screwed things up.

'Maybe I wasn't being very fair,' she said, swallowing away the lump in her throat and sniffing back the ever-threatening tears. 'I mean, there he was, expecting me to be agreeing to a fling, and I came out with a declaration of the for-ever kind of love. It's hardly surprising he was speechless. No wonder he didn't do anything. He was probably frozen in shock.'

'Could be,' said the man to her right, who nodded slowly and then drained his pint. 'Men don't tend to like surprises.'

'Not even good ones?' asked Abby.

'*Was* it a good one?' said the man to her left, for in the

half an hour she'd been in the pub the tales of her woes had gathered quite a crowd.

'Probably not,' she said sadly. 'But I can't go back. I've burned my bridges there. I really have.' She swiped a tear that had dared to spill over. 'And you know, for him I'd have totally been prepared to pretend not to know how to change a light bulb. I could have done that. I'm sure I could. But the truly, devastatingly ironic thing is I wouldn't have needed to.'

Another tear fell and her glass was topped up. 'Thank you,' she said and blew her nose.

'No problem,' said Sheila with a quick pat on her arm. 'I have no idea what you're talking about but if you ask me he doesn't deserve your tears. He sounds like all men. Crap.'

'I wish he was,' said Abby with a shaky sigh. 'But he isn't. So he's not perfect, but, you know what? Neither am I. I've always sought out perfection, but it doesn't exist because, actually, being perfect is a flaw too, isn't it?'

Sheila gave her an uncomprehending look.

'What I mean, I think, is that maybe a fling would have been enough. And maybe I ought to go back and tell him. Maybe I should just take what he has to offer because, you know, the alternative, which is never seeing him again, is just about breaking my heart. Maybe I should go now.' She glanced at the clock that hung over the bar. 'Or is two o'clock too late? I'm not sure I can wait, though.'

But then there was a hammering on the door and all thoughts of leaving shot from her head because there came a voice from beyond the entrance to the warm, cosy pub, and Abby went so dizzy she nearly fell off her stool.

'Open up!'

Everyone went deathly silent, as if taking a collective breath could somehow detract from the fact that they were all partaking of an illegal lock-in.

'Maybe it's the police,' said someone in a hushed voice from over by the fire.

'It can't be the police,' said someone else. '*I'm* the police.'

'It isn't the police,' said Abby, her voice sounding as though it came from far, far away and her heart beating so wildly she feared for her ribs.

Sheila's eyes widened. 'Is it *him*?'

She nodded, feeling as though she were having an out-of-body experience. 'I rather think it might be.'

'Heavens,' said Sheila, clasping a hand to her chest. 'Drama.'

But Abby shook her head as the shock receded and reality reappeared. 'He doesn't do drama. He's probably here with a query over my bill.'

'Will someone open this damned door,' shouted Leo, 'or do I have to break it down?'

'That definitely sounds like drama,' said Sheila, plucking a key off a hook and making her way to the door.

And she was right, it did, but Abby was going to remain icy calm because she wasn't going to read into his sudden appearance. She really wasn't.

But that didn't stop her heart from giving a stupid lurch when Sheila opened the door and there he was looking so intense, so dishevelled and so wild that her head spun.

His gaze darted around the pub, and, when it fell on her, pinned her to the spot. Not taking his eyes off her for even a second, he strode through the pub, a path appearing like the parting of the waves. He came to a stop right in front of her. So close and radiating so much heat and tension that she went dizzy all over again and had to grip the edges of her stool for support.

'What are you doing here?' she said and annoyingly enough it came out as a croaky whisper.

'You didn't give me a chance to respond.'

'Yes, I did.'

His eyes burned into hers and Abby's mouth went dry.

'About five seconds, Abby. Do you really think that was long enough?'

She swallowed and looked at him, and, goodness, it was hard not to reach out and touch. 'And if I'd given you longer?'

'That's why I'm here. I've had longer.'

'And?'

'You caught me by surprise, Abby, back there in the folly.'

'I know I did. I'm sorry.'

He swung his gaze around the room, over the thirty or so people dotted about the place not even bothering to pretend they weren't agog, and then back to Abby. 'Look, is there somewhere a bit more private we could do this?'

As the only option was her room, which was hardly appropriate given the way things stood, she shook her head. 'I'm afraid not.'

Leo's jaw tightened and he shifted as if uncomfortable, but then he shrugged and said, 'Fine. If that's the way it has to be.'

But apparently it wasn't because a second later Sheila was yelling, 'Make some space by the fire, people. Let's give these two a chance to talk,' and, with a few muttered protests, the sofa sitting in front of the fire was vacated.

Slipping off the stool, Abby arched an eyebrow at her. 'You've changed your tune.'

Sheila leaned forwards and said in a low voice, 'Yes, well, he's gorgeous, and he was willing to break down a door for you. I bet *he'd* never skive off child-support payments.'

'No, you're right, he wouldn't.'

And because he wouldn't and because she was desperate to know what he had to say, she let Leo take her hand and lead her to the sofa. They sat down. Waited for a moment for everyone to return their attention to their drinks and conversation, and just when Abby thought she was going to burst from the anticipation and longing and, above all, hope, Leo spoke.

'I owe you an explanation,' he said and she instantly felt like a balloon that had been popped because that wasn't what she'd been hoping for. At all.

'What about?' she said, struggling to keep the disappointment from her voice, her face.

'My wedding day.'

'I know about your wedding day.'

'No,' he said urgently. 'You don't know the half of it. You don't know what happened after Lisa left me at the altar. Hardly anyone does.'

'What happened, Leo?'

He swallowed, grimaced and an ache started up in her chest at the flicker of old pain that she saw in his eyes. 'I caught up with her outside the church,' he said, 'and I begged her to reconsider. Begged her. I loved her. I thought. So I threw aside my pride and told her everything I was feeling. And I mean, everything. All the emotions that were swirling around inside me, the pain, the jealousy, the hurt.' He winced. Sighed. Shook his head. 'It wasn't pretty,' he said hoarsely. 'In fact it was hideous. And even worse, it was witnessed. Not by everyone, but by Jake and a few other friends who'd dashed after me.'

Abby's heart squeezed. 'What happened after that?'

'I hated her for a while, especially the pity I'd seen on her face. But not for all that long, because despite the way it looks she's not a bitch. She was genuinely in bits over what she was doing,' he said, and then, with a shrug, 'but as she said at the time, she just couldn't do anything about it.'

Well, she could have done, thought Abby waspishly. She could have called it off the week before. The morning before even. She hadn't had to leave it until a moment that she must have known was going to destroy the man she'd once supposedly loved.

'I imagine the lure of a childhood sweetheart is a powerful thing,' she said instead.

'Maybe. Whatever it was, my heart had been absolutely shredded and every one of my emotions trampled on. And then when I'd got over the pain, I realised I'd been made to look like a fool. It wasn't something I was particularly keen to repeat.'

'No.'

'It was so easy just to lock the emotions down. That way I'd never be vulnerable or look a fool again. I'd be safe.' He stopped. Looked at her thoughtfully and smiled slightly. 'But then I met you and those intentions went straight to hell.'

'Oh, Leo.'

'There's no need to look like that. They're not locked down now. And I really don't give a toss about being vulnerable or looking like a fool.'

Her heart began to thump. 'No?'

'No. I mean, look at me. I'm a wreck and I'm spilling my guts in front of a pub full of people.' He glanced over, arched an eyebrow, and said to the room at large when gazes were hurriedly averted and conversation suddenly started up again, 'Oh, don't pretend you're not all trying your hardest to listen in.'

Then he turned back and the amusement in his eyes faded. 'I can't begin to tell you what I feel for you, Abby.'

Her breath caught at the look on his face. 'You can always try.'

'I love you. I adore you. I think I have done for weeks because, you know something, yes, that trip I organised to the *St Jude's* set might have had an ulterior motive, but you were right. I *did* want to do something nice for you. And I know you probably don't believe me, but I'll show you the emails I sent Caroline when I was trying to set up the meeting. They're embarrassingly gushy. They sing your praises and list your virtues. And there are lots. I love you, Abby. Very much. It's not just lust that I feel for you even though I managed to convince myself it was. It's love.'

Happiness soared through her and her heart swelled to bursting. 'As a first attempt,' she said shakily, 'that's not bad.'

He took a deep breath. 'The thing is, I'm also scared.'

'There's nothing to be scared of.'

'Oh, I think there is.'

'I'd never do anything to hurt you.'

'I know,' he said with a nod, 'but being in love with you also brings the terror of losing you.'

'You won't lose me.'

'Won't I?' he said, and the look in his eyes turned troubled. 'What if I turn out to be, I don't know, somehow not enough?'

Abby frowned. 'Not enough?' How could he possibly be not enough?

'I wasn't enough for Lisa—we'd been together for three years and she ran off with someone she'd been back in touch with for five minutes. I might not be enough for you.'

Ooh, if she ever got her hands on that woman...

'You are more than enough for me, Leo,' she said fervently. 'More than enough. You're everything I could ever want. Ever. How can I prove it to you?'

'You could kiss me and tell me you love me again. That would be a start.'

A second later she was scooting over to him, wrapping her arms around his neck and fitting her mouth to his. Kissing him hard and with everything she felt and, with what little of her brain that wasn't melting, thinking that it had been too, too long since they'd done this. It was so lovely, so thrilling, so scorchingly hot, and they were being watched. She could feel it. So she drew back reluctantly and looked deep into his eyes. 'I love you,' she said softly. 'Now, what else?'

'You could marry me.'

Her breath caught in her throat and her heart swelled. 'Are you sure?'

'I am if you promise to be there at the church and stick with me at the altar and beyond.'

'Oh, I do, I do.'

'Is that a yes?'

'Is that a proposal?'

'Absolutely.'

'Then yes, it's a yes.'

'I love you, Abby,' he said, putting his hands gently either side of her head and drawing her back to him.

'And I love you.'

She leaned in for another kiss, and, when the wolf whistles eventually filtered through the dizziness in her head, murmured against his mouth, 'Want to take this somewhere a bit more private, say my room?'

As his heart leapt beneath her hand and his eyes took on a wicked gleam, he smiled and said softly, 'I can think of nothing I'd like more.'

* * * * *